Contents

Complete Stories

p171

Poetry

p14

J. Campbell Kerr Paintings

p174

Dear Readers...

WELCOME to "The People's Friend" Annual 2014, which contains a feast of great reading for you! We have 25 brand-new stories from many of your favourite "Friend" authors for you to enjoy from the comfort of your favourite armchair.

We also have 15 seasonal poems for you, as well as some nostalgic snippets from 50 years ago, which we hope will bring back many fond memories.

You might recognise some of our wonderful J. Campbell Kerr paintings, which will take you on a scenic trip round the UK.

We're sure you'll love this year's Annual, but if you want some more super reading, there are plenty of heartwarming stories and fascinating features every week in "The People's Friend" magazine – a weekly treat for the whole family!

Your Editor

Cheek To Cheek

by Pamela Ormondroyd.

EVERYBODY wants to dance with Malcolm. But if you don't get along to Malcolm's Dancing School dead on the dot on a Monday, you might not get a look in, because I guarantee he'll be booked up solid.

He has the knack, you see, our Malcolm. That lovely way of making his partners feel so special. He whisks them around the floor like they are floating on air, and for those few precious moments, in Malcolm's arms, you might be Ginger Rogers or Cyd Charisse . . . or anyone you choose.

He's dancing the quickstep with Ruby Catchpole when Ivy and I get there. The couple are revolving round the parquet floor, shoulders balanced, straight backs and stiff arms. Yet their movement is all light and bouncy, like they're dancing on hot coals.

I'll say this for Ruby, she always makes an effort. Dolled up to the nines, she is, in that pink silk dress with the thousand sequins that her mum sewed on by hand.

"Not a bad turn-out for a Monday," Ivy says, looking round. She opens the kitchen shutters and I knock the switch on the tea urn. The battered old machine, slowly and begrudgingly, flickers into life.

"Mind you, there are a lot of females in tonight. Your Malcolm will be shattered by the end of the evening!"

I nod and open the cupboard, and start putting cups and plastic beakers on the counter.

"I wonder if Mac and Louie will be in tonight. If they are, we might get a last waltz out of them if we're lucky."

"Or we'll have to dance it with each other again." Ivy smiles.

MAC and Louie are twins. They live in a bungalow at the back of our flats and we've known them for ages. Mac's a bit of a rogue. By all accounts, he was a proper ladies' man when he was younger. Or, as Ivy would say, a wolf!

Louie is quieter and a more educated gentleman, well-read and well-spoken, who doffs his cap and then pulls your seat out for you when you sit down. He's taken a bit of a shine to our Ivy, but she won't have any of it . . . even though, secretly, I know she's a little bit flattered.

The quickstep has ended and over the top of the box of crisps on the counter I can see that Rhona Simpson is having a word. Malcolm nods and changes the record.

This should be interesting – it's the rumba, one of Malcolm's favourites. To the delight of his lady admirers he does a quick demonstration, swaying his

Illustration by Len Thurston.

flexible hips and flashing his pearl-white teeth. Rhona Simpson finally grabs him and together the pair swing and sway about the hall, a little too close for comfort, in my opinion.

Mac might be the neighbourhood wolf, but it's Rhona who's a bit of a man-eater. She's attractive and curvy and makes a good dancing partner, and she's not slow in coming forward, if you know what I mean. Nor am I struck on the slinky skirt she's got on. It's far too tight.

"Got any cola, Mrs Grimshaw?"

Young Toby Foster, one of Malcolm's protégés, peeks over the kitchen counter. Only sixteen, but he's a great little mover. In fact, Malcolm reckons that Toby and his partner, Lena, are so rhythmically suited that they have all the makings of being junior champions next year.

I fetch a large bottle of pop out of the store room and pour him a beaker full.

"What about Lena?" I ask, looking round the hall. "Hasn't she turned up yet?"

"Oh, Lena's not coming tonight." Toby looks around with sadness in his eyes. "I don't think she'll be coming back any other night, either."

"Why's that, then?" Ivy pours milk into a jug.

"We've split up, that's why." Toby scowls. "I suppose I'll have to look for another dancing partner now."

He goes off to drown his sorrows with his cola and a bag of crisps.

"That's a shame," Ivy says as the tea urn starts to bubble and hiss like a venomous snake. "I don't know what Malcolm will say."

The music changes to a foxtrot and everyone glides around the room, trying to follow Malcolm's instructions. He's dancing with Miss Plumb now, a retired maths teacher, who leans heavily on his slim shoulder and treads on his toes. But Malcolm's a professional in the true sense of the word and, however many times his bunion is stamped on, he knows the show must go on.

Mac and Louie turn up at this point.

"Why, it's our little harem!" Mac says with a twinkle in his eye.

Louie takes off his cap.

"Good evening, ladies."

"We've been teaching ourselves the salsa!" Mac looks pleased with himself. "Me and Louie have been practising nearly all week."

"Not in that little bungalow of yours?" I say, trying not to laugh. "That must have been a sight for sore eyes."

"Well, we had to move some of the furniture," Mac conceded. "But we went outside into the garden when it was fine."

"But it's a communal garden!" Ivy looks aghast. "What about the neighbours?"

Louie shakes his head forlornly.

"Anyway, we're not bad at it, you know," Mac goes on. "Not bad at all. We'll take you ladies for a spin on the floor in a bit, if you like."

"Sorry. Hips are playing up. But Ivy will have a dance with Louie, won't you, love?"

Poor Ivy. Her face turns bright red and she looks at me, flummoxed.

"I don't know about that."

Luckily, the music stops for a while and everyone comes hurrying across to the kitchen, Mac and Louie getting lost in the stampede.

W E'RE nearing the end of the evening now. All the cups have been washed, dried and put away and Malcolm is dancing the tango with PC Jenkins, our local community support officer. She's a lovely girl, that one. Only in her twenties, and very pretty, with long golden hair that only ever sees the light of day when she's off duty.

She and Malcolm make the perfect dancing couple. She's keen and learns quickly, and she gets completely into the character of the dance. Tonight, she and Malcolm are making those difficult, sharp tango movements quite expertly, keeping their shape and expression spot on. Just like his father and I used to do it, oh, 40 years ago.

Over in the corner, skinny, pale-faced Toby is having an almighty struggle with the portly Miss Plumb. Oh, the lady's expression is well suited to the tango, of course – staid, and cement-like as always. It suits Toby's miserable countenance well, but unfortunately that's where any hint of synchronisation bites the dust!

At the back of the room, we notice Mac and Louie are practising what look like their salsa moves. Ivy says they look like they've both been doused in itching powder and we both collapse in fits of giggles.

We are still wiping our eyes when we notice a figure standing in the doorway, a slim, very sweet-looking girl who looks anxious and a little tearful. It's Lena.

When Toby sees her he stops in his tracks, almost dropping Miss Plumb on to the parquet. The pair stare across at each other for a moment or two and then Toby walks over. They chat for a minute and then they go out into the cloakroom area.

The last waltz comes on and I still have a few things to attend to in the kitchen, but Ivy is asked by Louie to dance, and I notice they chat happily all through the number.

I wave to Mac, who puts on a pretend glum face, but he seems to be enjoying himself with slinky Rhona Simpson, so I don't feel too bad.

I POP into the cloakroom to fetch our coats and catch a peek of Toby and Lena. They are performing their own cheek-to-cheek waltz in a little dark, quiet alcove, so I reckon that that particular lovers' tiff has already been resolved. It'll be nice to see them back again next Monday.

"'Night, everyone, see you all next week!" Malcolm waves to our local bobby, then switches off the main lights.

Ivy looks quite pleased with herself. She's going to some book club with Louie tomorrow. I told you they were well suited, didn't I?

"Right, well, everything's off, Mum," Malcolm says as we head for the door. "A good night, I reckon."

Yes, I smile to myself. Very good and most entertaining all round.

I'm glad I didn't sell up when the dancing school got a bit much for me. I was always hoping that our son would one day take over the ropes, and he has.

And it's nice still to feel a part of everything even though the old bones don't do what they should these days.

Good music, company, glamour, drama, laughs. It's all on tap, at Malcolm's School of Dancing! ∎

Illustration by David Axtell.

A Garden
Of Hope

by Heather Pardoe.

HE came out of nowhere. Cassie Helyer gasped as firm hands gripped the handlebars of her bicycle, easing it to a stop. "Quickly," the man said, his voice low and urgent. "Get into the shadow of the tree. Hurry."

He was accustomed to command. She could hear it in his firm tone, one that was both reassuring and impossible to disobey.

Cassie slid swiftly from her seat, thankful that she had risked not changing back into her skirt for the ride home under cover of darkness from Appleford Farm that evening.

Whatever the village gossips might say, it was far easier to disentangle herself from the bicycle and run while still wearing her brother William's cut-down trousers, rather than encumbered by the heavy material of her skirt.

It was a clear, moonless night, with just the sheen of stars to guide her to the large oak tree at the side of the road, where the high stone walls of Roseland Hall began.

"What is it?" she whispered, turning as he joined her, the precious bicycle abandoned in the grass.

"It must be lost," he replied, breathing hard, one hand on the trunk of the tree to steady himself. "Or turning back, and looking for a place to jettison its incendiaries. I hope to heaven there are no lights showing in the village tonight."

Cassie's heart clenched. Port Helen had been her home for all her life. Everyone she had ever known and loved lived in the little cottages tucked into the shelter of the bay. It had always felt so safe, so far away from outside harm.

There was the sea, of course, with its ever-present danger of the storms that swept in across the Cornish coast. Every family from the village had at least one young man away at the Front, but the war itself had still seemed far away.

She peered through the bare branches above her as a shadow loomed slowly above them, blocking out the stars.

"It's huge!" she whispered in awe.

"I thought it looked low," her companion replied. "No Zeppelin can stay airborne at that altitude. It must have developed a fault."

CARRIE shivered. There were men up there in the great bulbous shape drifting over their heads. Enemy they might be, but they were still human beings.

"We'd better get inside the walls," her rescuer said. "If that thing comes down close by . . ." He left the sentence hanging in the air. "Go ahead, the gate is open. We can fetch your bicycle afterwards," he added as she hesitated.

The Zeppelin seemed even lower, almost as if it could touch the highest branches of the tree. Cassie shot through the wooden gate and into the Roselands' garden.

But this time her rescuer was not so fast. Cassie came to a halt as she reached the large water trough just inside the door. Had he gone to rescue her

11

bicycle? Or had he stayed to watch where the airborne craft came down?

The next minute there was the tap of wood on stone, and the man swung himself through, a crutch under each arm.

"It looks like it's attempting to come down on the beach," he remarked. "At least the tide's far enough out still. They might stand a chance, poor devils, if the thing doesn't burst into flames on impact."

He swung himself closer in, more awkwardly now as he reached uneven ground. In the starlight, she could make out the heavy bandaging on his left leg.

"I'll close the door," she said hastily.

"No need," he retorted, pushing the door smartly to with a crutch. "I'm not entirely helpless."

"I didn't mean that. I was only trying to help."

"I know." His tone softened. "I'm sorry. I'm not accustomed to asking for assistance."

T HEY stood for a while in silence, ears straining for any sound of the Zeppelin's fate.

"What's your name?" he asked at last.

"Cassie. Cassie Helyer."

"Pleased to meet you, Cassie Helyer. I'm Edward Miller." She could sense him attempting to make out her face in the darkness. "There was a housemaid called Helyer up at the Hall, when the Roseland family still lived here before the war."

She nodded.

"That would be my sister, Marie."

"Marie. Yes, that was it. Marie Helyer. Didn't she go to work in a munitions factory in Portsmouth?"

"She's still there."

"And preferring it to working for the Roselands, I expect."

"Yes," Cassie replied a little uncertainly. "Well, not the work, of course, but it's better paid than being a housemaid, and she has much more free time to lead her own life. She's sharing a house with some other girls from Port Helen."

"Good for her. Your sister was always far too lively to spend her days and nights trapped in a crumbling old place like this."

"But it's only for a short while. Just while the war's on," Cassie protested. "Once the soldiers return things will go back to normal."

"Will they?" His profile showed a long, thin face with a prominent nose. She could make out the glint of his eyes. "Is that what you want?"

"I don't know." She had never really considered it, Cassie admitted to herself.

She loved the work on the farm, being out in the fresh air, feeling her body

Fifty Years Ago . . .

January 11, 1964

FIFTY years ago the iconic teenage magazine "Jackie" hit the streets. Appearing weekly, it ran until July 3, 1993 – 1534 issues.

A best-seller for 10 years, it featured fashion, beauty, celebrity gossip, a problem page, true-life photo stories and fiction – where the girl always finished up with the boy of her dreams!

Pop idols were a favourite and the centre poster was designed to be pulled out and put on the wall. There must have been barely a girl's bedroom in the UK that did not feature a "Jackie" poster. Favourite pop stars included David Cassidy, Donny Osmond, Marc Bolan, David Essex and Michael Jackson. At certain times of the year readers were treated to a free gift which could vary from a heart-shaped photo frame to a tail comb or sachet of shampoo. The first issue, shown above, gave away a Twin Heart ring which no teenager could be without!

Readers wrote in to the magazine in their hundreds, with the agony aunts in particular receiving sackfuls of mail. To a great many teenagers of the 60s, 70s and 80s it really was a girl's best friend. It is still regarded with affection by many women today. ∎

Every Thursday, Jan. 11, 1964

Jackie
for go·ahead teens

Nº1

FREE TWIN HEART RING

SUPER FULL COLOUR PIN-UPS OF CLIFF, ELVIS, BILLY FURY and The **BEATLES**

PERFUME TIPS FOR A MORE KISSABLE YOU

DREAMY PICTURE LOVE STORIES

COLOUR PICTURES OF OUTFITS TO MAKE YOU PRETTY IN THE RAIN 'N' SNOW

PHOTO FEATURES AND WAY-OUT EXCLUSIVES ON ALL THE POPSTERS

grow stronger by the day, her hands deep in the earth. But it had always seemed a temporary state of affairs. Like the war.

"I hated it when I was working up at the Hall," she admitted.

"When were you there?"

"For a few months just after the war started."

"Ah," he said, as if that explained something. "I'd have left by then."

"Left?"

"For the Front. The other gardeners were joining up, so I went, too. It seemed the right thing to do, and it was only for a few months. 'Over by Christmas' – isn't that what they used to say?"

"Yes," Cassie agreed.

In the distance, from the direction of Port Helen, the alarm sounded, echoing through the still air.

"Ah, I told the men to alert the authorities. At least they'll be on their way to rescue the crew by now."

Cassie shuddered. Surrounded by the walls and the shadow of the house, the Zeppelin could no longer be seen, but she could hear the stutter of the engine, which came briefly into life, then faded as the craft sank below the cliffs.

"You were a gardener here, then?" she asked hastily. There was nothing

A Fresh Start

THE daylight hours are lengthening,
In this, another year,
We've travelled back from Bethlehem,
Curtailed our Christmas cheer.
Those New Year's resolutions
We're trying hard to keep,
Knowing deep down in our hearts
That what we sow, we'll reap.

– *Don Robinson.*

Thinkstockphotos.

either of them could do, and she had an urgent need to keep her mind from bracing itself for the crash.

"Yes." Edward seemed lost in thought. "It's all I ever wanted to be. My uncle worked his way up to be under-gardener for Lord Roseland before the war. This kitchen garden was his pride and joy. He always said I had the knack, and that one day I might even make it to become head gardener."

He adjusted himself on his crutches.

"That seems a lifetime ago now. Lord Roseland sent the family to America once the Hall was to be used for wounded soldiers. With no gardeners here to tend to it, the garden has been left to rack and ruin since I've been away. Who knows if any of them will ever return?"

A muffled thud filled the air, followed by the screech and crash of the Zeppelin finally hitting the sands. In front of them, the house erupted into life. The front door swung open, along with several of the shuttered windows on the first floor, allowing the unnaturally bright glow of electric light to spill out into the darkness, accompanied by rushing figures and the excited chatter of voices.

O N the highest point of the house, where the slope of the roof met the tiny attic window of the servants' quarters, torchlight streaked into the night, lighting up faces as it passed.

"Did you see that?" A small group of men were rushing along the paths towards them, torches held high. "Did you see that, Captain? Only just missed the house, it did. Blasted great –"

Edward cleared his throat loudly.

"Oh!" The torch was lifted higher, revealing a rounded face beneath a heavy swathe of bandages. "Beg pardon, miss. I didn't see you there." Sharp blue eyes moved from Cassie to Edward and back again with undisguised curiosity.

"I'd better go," Cassie muttered, feeling a blush rise up from her collar. "Thank you for ensuring I was safe, Captain Miller, but my family will be wondering where I am, and I don't want to leave my bicycle by the side of the road any longer."

"You can't go now, miss," the soldier exclaimed before Edward could even open his mouth. "Me and the lads are off to see if we can lend a hand. That Zeppelin came down in one piece. There could be half-a-dozen Germans roaming the countryside by now, armed to the teeth –"

"That'll do, Edwards," Edward broke in sharply. "There's no point in terrifying Miss Helyer. All the same," he added, turning back to Cassie, "I don't think we should leave you to go down to Port Helen on your own."

"I'm not afraid."

"I'm sure you aren't. But there will be a lot of jittery people out there tonight, no doubt armed with any weapon they can lay their hands on and in no mood to ask questions first." He coughed. "And, um, if you'll forgive me saying so, it isn't immediately obvious you are a woman. I assumed myself you were one of the village lads or I'd never have stopped you quite so roughly."

"Oh." Cassie became aware of more men arriving, the light from their torches leaving her trousers nowhere to hide.

"If anything happened, none of us would ever forgive ourselves," Edward added, pressing home his advantage. "There will be plenty of vehicles making their way back to Port Helen before long. So if you could rescue Miss Helyer's bicycle on the way, Edwards . . ."

"But my mother –" Cassie began.

"There's a telephone installed up at Roselands. I'm sure the Port Helen police will send a boy to let your family know you are safe."

"Thank you," Cassie murmured as they made their way up to the house.

THE sun was shining as Cassie propped her bicycle against the walls of Roseland Hall a few days later, before making her way through the wooden gate.

As she began to follow the path towards the house, she discovered Captain Miller propped on his crutches, gazing deep in thought at one of the weed-filled vegetable beds.

"Hello," she said shyly.

Edward started, as if brought back from far away.

"Hello," he replied, turning towards her, a slow smile lightening the seriousness of his face.

"I was passing on my way home," Cassie explained. "I wanted to thank you for arranging for my bicycle to be returned to me. And for all the work you did on it. It works much better now than it ever did."

And it shone, too. She had scarcely recognised her rusty old bicycle as the gleaming machine that had appeared outside the cottage the morning after the drama of the crashed Zeppelin. There had barely been room for her in the motor vehicle of the local doctor, crammed already with nurses, when Captain Miller had persuaded Dr Adams to take her home. There had certainly been no room for a bicycle with its pannier full of cabbages for soup, and its wheels covered in mud.

Edward's smile broadened. That's how he must have been, she thought: it was a glimpse back to the lighthearted young man, passionately ensuring the Roselands vines and exotic pineapples grew to their utmost perfection. The young man he had been before the war came.

"It was my pleasure," he replied. "I'm not very good at staying still, I'm afraid." He prodded the earth with a crutch. "If only this cursed leg of mine would heal. I should be back with my men, or at least getting this garden back into shape." She could hear the frustration in his voice.

"With all the food shortages, it's a crime this is just being left to rot. But now they are saying I'll need another operation. That'll be like going back to the day I was injured again, with months before I can walk."

"I'm sorry." She hovered, not quite certain what to say.

"No, no." His smile broke through again. "I'm the one who should be sorry. I'm being selfish. There are so many far worse off than I. I should be grateful for what I have, and the doctors say I have every chance of a full recovery." He prodded at the earth with his crutch once more.

"I just hate not being able to do my bit." He gave a wry grunt. "I couldn't even help pull those Germans from the Zeppelin to safety."

"But you saved them." Cassie frowned at him. "Doctor Adams said you're the one who called him and the fire truck, and arranged for all the able-bodied men to go and help He told us it was your quick thinking that meant that even the injured survived and were all got to safety before the tide came in."

"Hrmph." He was back to gazing at the earth once more.

Cassie took a deep breath.

"Why shouldn't it be the same with this garden?"

His crutch paused.

"You mean, tell others what to do?"

"You have the skills and the knowledge. That's the part that takes years to gain. Others can dig and do what you tell them. You can pass your skills on."

B
UT who to?" His voice was despairing, but the crutch had remained still. "The men here are in no fit shape for heavy work, and all the able-bodied men of the village are either in France or undertaking war work. Everyone I see is exhausted from overwork and worry, not to mention the lack of food."

"I'll help," Cassie said stoutly. "And the other girls from the farm will, too. And there are the children."

"Children?"

"My sister Anna is a teacher at Port Helen School. She was saying only last week that plenty of schoolchildren all over the country are helping with growing food in school grounds and even along the sides of roads; anywhere they can."

"Schoolchildren." He still sounded unconvinced.

"Just because it isn't something big or dangerous or glorious doesn't mean it doesn't matter," Cassie said. "Anna says that's where the war will really be won or lost: if there's not enough food to keep everyone going and give them the strength to do what they need to do, then we cannot survive, let alone win. I know it's not as dangerous or nearly so horrible, but in its own way it's a battlefield here, too."

"With women and children as soldiers," he replied with a wry smile.

"Oh, and do you think we can't be?" she retorted. "Or are you one of those people who think women shouldn't be given the vote?"

"Of course not!" He was indignant. "I have always supported the suffragette cause. My sisters would never let me hear the last of it otherwise," he added with a grin.

Cassie laughed, and suddenly Edward was chuckling, too.

"Well?" Cassie asked.

"I'll need to speak to Lord Roseland, of course." He pulled his crutch from the earth back on to the path, and limped a few steps nearer. "But I think I should be able to manage a regiment of women and children, even if it is from my hospital bed," he said.

OVER the next months, the kitchen garden of Roselands Hall was transformed. The operation to remove the remainder of the shrapnel in Captain Miller's leg was pronounced a success and within weeks he was insisting on being wheeled out to direct operations from the wheelchair he had commandeered for the purpose.

Between helping her mother and her work at the farm, Cassie spent as much time as she could at Roselands.

Despite the long walk to and from the village, the children worked wonders, removing weeds and digging and planting with enthusiasm. As word got about, they were joined by some of the old men, and the boys waiting to be called up, along with women of all ages who could spare an hour or so between tending their families and undertaking the work of the missing men on the fishing boats and the fields.

As spring passed, Edward's leg began to heal. By the time the long days of summer came, he had even left his crutches behind and was walking with a stick, joining in with the tending of the plants in the garden and the greenhouses.

That year, no-one in Port Helen went hungry. Carrots and potatoes jostled with the dark bulbs and leafy stems of beetroot and the bright green of peas in their shiny pods as the children returned home with fresh vegetables, plenty for every family.

They even had enough to store. Cassie spent a week with some of the older children clearing out the old storage sheds ready for sacks of potatoes, and long strings of onions hung up cool and dry.

A corner of the Roseland kitchens had already been commandeered for bottling, pickling and jam making of every fruit and vegetable that wasn't immediately eaten.

"It didn't do them too much harm, being pruned so late," Edward remarked one afternoon as they finally began to turn their attention to the laden branches of the apple orchard.

"Not in the least," Cassie said. She made sure she sounded cheerful, despite the hard squeezing of her heart in her chest. She had never seen Edward in his uniform before. He looked handsome, but also somehow remote, as if he didn't belong in the gardens any more.

"I'll be sure to prune them earlier next year," he remarked.

"Yes," Cassie replied, her throat dry, her voice barely a whisper.

"And if by any chance I'm not here, then I'm sure you'll remember the way I showed you."

"Yes," Cassie replied. "I'll always remember."

"I'm glad," he said. He turned to meet her eyes, as if about to say something more, but at that moment a group of children arrived to gather the windfalls around their feet.

Cassie could hear the sound of an automobile engine starting up. She swallowed hard.

"You'd better go," she said.

Slowly, he nodded. Then with a smile and a wave he was gone, striding towards the house with barely a limp at all.

*   *   *   *

It was a bright spring morning as Cassie approached the grounds of Roseland Hall. Frost still hung on the ivy and glimmered on the yellow primroses nestled beneath the walls. She slowed the bicycle to a standstill, jumping off and pushing it slowly past, her skirt slapping against her legs and catching on the pedals.

The Gardener's Year

SPRINGTIME can often be hectic,
There's always a great deal to do,
There's digging and planting and sowing of seeds,
As the cycle of growth starts anew.

In summer our flowers are a picture,
But there is still lots to be done,
There's watering, weeding and mowing the lawn,
Before we relax in the sun.

In autumn the spoils of our labours
In orchard and garden abound,
We feel so content as we harvest the crops
That we've grown in our own bit of ground.

In winter there's time for a breather,
Although there are still things to do.
And while we're relaxing we draw up our plans
For the year that is starting anew.

– Rosemary Bennett.

She would miss the planting this year, the watching of the fruit and vegetables growing beneath the sheltering walls of the kitchen garden. Even though the war was at last over, there were still shortages of food.

But the Roseland family were moving back, and things were returning to the way they had always been. And today was her last day at the farm.

The men who had returned from the war needed jobs. Not that she minded, after all they had been through and all the sacrifices they had made. She was lucky enough to have the prospect of a job herself, with the Roselands. But her heart still sank as she paused at the gate to the kitchen garden, looking around at the first shoots of green springing from the earth.

"Cassie!"

She swung round.

"Edward? Captain Miller, I mean."

"Well, Major, actually," he replied with a grin. "But Edward will do. Lord Roseland said you were coming for an interview here today."

"Oh, yes," Cassie said. He hadn't changed. Older. Thinner. A little more lined. But still the same Edward Miller. Her heart seemed to have stopped in her chest. "There's a position as a laundry maid."

"I bet there is," he replied. "And barely an applicant."

"So I've heard," Cassie said. She could hear the gloom in her own voice.

"Well, they'd better round up some more," Edward said.

Cassie blinked.

"But –"

"You don't really have a burning ambition to be a laundry maid, do you?"

"Of course not!" She glared at him.

"GOOD." For some reason he was smiling. "Because I've bought Brook Farm, just over the way there, overlooking the sea, and I've a far better proposition in mind."

Cassie frowned.

"You won't be popular if you're proposing to employ women when there are so many men in need of work."

His smile broadened.

"Well, I was considering someone to work with me to run the farm. But I wasn't exactly thinking of an employee." He had taken a step closer and his arms were slowly making their way around her waist.

"I know you'll need time to think it over, but I was wondering – hoping – that one day you might consider being my wife."

Cassie stood quite still. She could feel the gentle warmth of the sun stealing through the clouds on to her, and breathed deep into her lungs the scent of warming earth and the new life around her.

"Yes," she replied, turning to meet his kiss. ■

Ae Fond Kiss

by Kate Blackadder.

FIVE to one. Time to go, if she was going.

Mary looked around at the tables with the green-checked cloths and pretty cream china, the blackboard listing all the delights on offer, and the quirky pictures on the walls. Even after six months she found it hard to believe that Mary's Place was finally open – the café she and her friend, Susan, had spent so much time planning. She couldn't imagine doing anything she liked more than feeding hungry tourists and office workers on Edinburgh's George IV Bridge.

Two students were huddled over bowls of soup, an elderly gentleman was having tea and scones at the other table by the window, and there was a small queue for take-away sandwiches. Nothing Susan couldn't cope with.

Would that young man who had been in at one o'clock every day this week come in today, Mary wondered. It would be a pity to miss him, she thought, recalling his brown eyes and shy smile. According to Susan, Mary had positively pushed her out of the way on his third day so that she could have the pleasure of making his chicken and avocado wrap.

The café was just round the corner from St Giles, but the event to take place outside Edinburgh's famous cathedral at one o'clock would only last a few minutes, and she'd promised Dad back home in Ayrshire that she'd get there if she possibly could. Even if it happened again it wouldn't be for a whole year.

She picked up her warm jacket.

"Susan, I'm just popping round to St Giles. Will you be OK?"

Her business partner looked up from the baguette she was stuffing with hummus and roasted vegetables.

"I think I can handle it." She laughed. "Have fun."

Illustration by Mike Heslop.

21

Outside, the sky was blue and the sun was shining, but it was bitterly cold. Mary drew her collar closely around her neck as she hurried round the corner.

A large number of folk were already gathered in Parliament Square, all taking a few minutes to celebrate the birthday of Scotland's most famous poet. Mary went to stand at the end of the back row.

When she'd heard about the forthcoming "flash mob" Mary had phoned her father. He'd always been a Burns admirer, and when his only child was born on January 25 he'd named her after the Bard's great love.

"A flash what?" he'd asked.

Mary, who'd only just heard the expression herself, explained.

"It's when a group of people get together at short notice and give a performance. This one is to sing 'My Love Is Like A Red, Red Rose'."

"I wish I could be there, but you tell me all about it," Dad had said. "How's the café?" he went on. "Any chance of you coming down for a weekend? You were looking so tired at Christmas. You should take some time off."

"Dad, I can't. We will look for someone to help part-time, but we can't afford it at the moment. I'm fine. Don't worry."

"I'm your father. I'm allowed to worry," he replied. "We worry that you're all work and no play at the moment."

Mary grinned to herself. This was tactful Dad-speak for "you haven't got a boyfriend".

"No time for play," she replied airily. "If Robert Burns himself appeared and wanted to give me 'ae fond kiss' I'd have to tell him to call back in a few years."

Mary remembered that conversation now as someone welcomed the "mob" and told them that song sheets were about to be given out.

IT was all too true. She had no time for anything but work. After a day spent on her feet all she wanted was an early night. That is, apart from the nights when she stayed up late to wrestle with the accounts or, with Susan, to experiment with soup recipes and sandwich fillings. Going out with friends, swimming and reading novels were all pleasures she'd put on hold for what seemed like the foreseeable future.

But here was the young man with the brown eyes giving her his shy smile as he came to stand next to her.

"Oh, hello," she said before she could stop herself.

"You're from the café round the corner, aren't you?" he said.

"Mary's Place," she replied, the saleswoman in her coming to the fore. "Good sandwiches!"

A girl was handing Mary a song sheet.

"I'm sorry. We didn't expect so many folk. Do you mind sharing?"

"No, of course not." Mary held out the sheet so that the brown-eyed man could take one side of it.

He smiled his thanks, but as Burns's lovely song rang out through the

22

frosty air, she realised that he wasn't looking at the sheet. He knew the words off by heart.

And then it was finished – a "flash" performance indeed.

There were some mutterings about singing "Auld Lang Syne" as well, but instead people began to drift away back to their warm homes and offices.

SOON only Mary and the man were left, still holding the song sheet. "I have to get back. I've left my colleague holding the fort." Mary spoke first.

"I haven't had any lunch yet. I'll come with you. Is Mary your name?"

Mary stuffed the song sheet into her jacket pocket.

"That's me. Dad's a great Burns man. So as I share his birthday he called me after Highland Mary." She glanced up at her companion as they walked round the corner. "I hope I have a longer and happier life than she did, though." She laughed.

"I hope you do, too," he said. He held open the door of the café for her.

"Do you want to sit in or take away?" Mary asked.

"I think I'll sit in today. I've got a meeting but it's not until two."

Their best table was free now.

"Why don't you sit by the window?" Mary said and she took his order then went through to the back room to hang up her jacket.

As Mary waited for the brie and cranberry panini to toast, Susan nudged her. "Who's your friend then?"

"Don't know his name," Mary said without moving her lips.

"Well, sit down with him and find out. I don't think he'll object from the way he's looking at you."

Thinkstockphotos.

Silent Friends

BOOKS are special kinds of friends,
In fact, they are unique;
They tell us all we want to know
Through words that never speak.

They can be dropped along the way,
But never seem to mind!
And to the questions puzzling us
The answers we shall find.

Books speak volumes, in their way,
Each word exactly meant;
Well-versed, of course, in happiness
And full of deep content.

– Elizabeth Gozney.

Mary cut the panini in two, added some green salad to the plate and took it over.

"Thank you, that looks good." He looked up at her. "So, today's your birthday. Are you doing anything special?"

Mary hesitated, then took Susan's advice and pulled out the other chair.

N OT special, but important. VAT returns," she said with a mock grimace. "I never dreamed there would be so much paperwork involved with running a café."

He put down his fork.

"You can't do accounts on your birthday!"

"They have to be done and they take me so long. Anyway, did you enjoy the flash mob?"

He nodded.

"My office is on the Royal Mile so I couldn't resist joining in when I realised what was happening. I was on my way here, in fact, when I saw you."

"It's funny when you see people out of context."

"I'd have recognised you anywhere." His smile was more confident now.

Mary felt herself go pink.

"Your panini's getting cold."

He didn't seem to care about that.

"We don't know each other, but we do have the Bard in common. I think that's a good introduction," he said. "I'm going to a Burns Supper tonight. Would you like to forget about VAT returns and come with me?"

"But I don't have a ticket," Mary pointed out.

"I'm on the organising committee," he said. "So that won't be a problem."

"But I . . . I don't even know your name."

He leaned forward.

"You'll never believe it, Highland Mary, but it's Rabbie Burns."

"No! Really?"

"No, not really." Now his smile was teasing her. He held out his hand. "It's Alex Mitchell."

"Well, thank you, Alex Mitchell. I'd love to."

Her response must have made his appetite come back because he released her hand and picked up his fork again.

"I have some experience of doing VAT returns," he said between bites. "I could give you a hand with them, if you like."

"That's the nicest thing anyone ever said to me." Mary laughed.

"I can't believe that," Alex said, and the look in his eyes made Mary blush again.

Whether the evening would end with "ae fond kiss" she could only speculate but as Alex dashed off, late for his meeting, he was humming a tune, telling the world that his love was like a red, red rose. ∎

Play Your Cards Right

by Celia K. Andrew.

G ILLIAN AMBROSE twiddled the sign on the shop door so that it read *Open* at exactly one minute to nine. She ran her fingers down the edges of the latest line of cards, wondering what it would be like to receive something as over the top as one of these beribboned, velvety creations.

Picking one of them up, she read the message and then the inside sentiment. She smiled, remembering fondly, and then sighed. Her time for Valentine cards was over. Her gaze slid over to the "Big 40" section and she grimaced. Her time for that, however, was fast approaching.

"Would you like a party?" her sister, at whose suggestion Gillian had moved back to Devon last year to be nearer the family, had asked.

"Oh, I don't think so. I don't much feel like celebrating."

"Well, at least come over for the weekend. The twins would love to try to bake you a cake. It's only two weeks away; we ought to make plans."

"I'd rather just let it go quietly, Mandy. Thanks anyway."

"It's been five years, Gill. You've got to move on. I know you've got the job now, but you've no social life."

"Don't worry about me. I'm all right as I am."

And mostly, she was. Gillian had a job she enjoyed, and was her own boss much of the time, since the owner of the little high street shop owned another in Tiverton and worked mainly there.

She had her dear little flat in a converted country house a few miles into the hills, where her passion for sketching, photography and walking could be indulged whenever five o'clock came and that notice was twiddled back to *Closed* for the night.

The bell pinged as a customer came in. It was one of her regulars, the farmer in the blue Land-Rover again. He came into town on Thursdays for the farmers' market. Middle-aged, average height and dark-haired, he seemed to have an enormous family for here he was again, going over the birthday cards, looking perplexed.

Gillian put down the card she had been reading and went back to the till to unpack some humorous Valentines. A bit close to the mark, some of the jokes, but at least they made her laugh. She pushed her glasses higher on to the bridge of her nose and looked up as the man approached.

I'LL have this one, please."

He had chosen a jokey card with a puppy on the front. The punchline was something about loo roll and puddles, and Gillian remembered laughing when she had put it on the display.

"Let me guess," she said, taking his money and ringing it in. "Thirteen, mad about dogs, sense of humour. And you get on with her really well." She smiled at him, their eyes almost level across the glass-topped counter.

"My daughter, twelve." He smiled slowly back. "And a yes to your other three assumptions."

They both chuckled as Gillian bagged the card and handed him his change.

"She's getting a puppy for her birthday," he volunteered.

In the few months he'd been coming into the shop, he'd bought a dozen cards for various members of his family and they had shared small-talk over the last five. Gillian found him so painfully shy that it pleased her to try to get him to talk a little more each time. It was like getting close enough to the wild deer on the moor to be able to photograph them.

"What kind of puppy?" she asked.

"Oh, a collie, of course," he answered, taking the bag and pleating the end over, scraping it flat with strong, weatherworn hands.

26

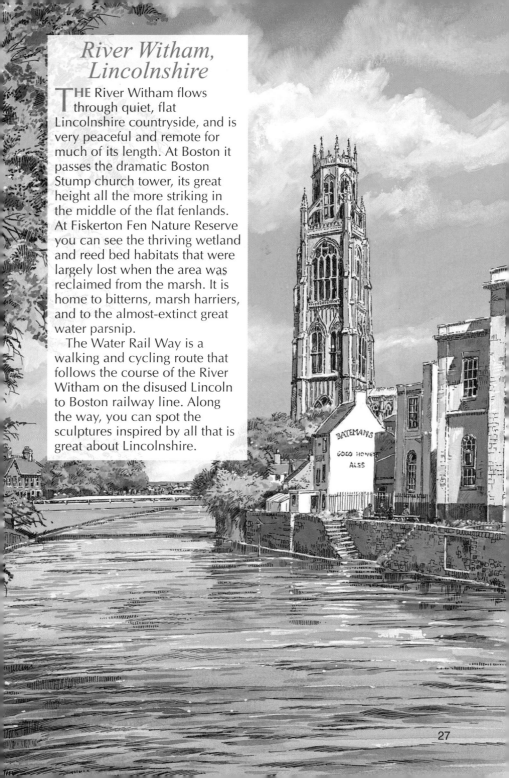

River Witham, Lincolnshire

THE River Witham flows through quiet, flat Lincolnshire countryside, and is very peaceful and remote for much of its length. At Boston it passes the dramatic Boston Stump church tower, its great height all the more striking in the middle of the flat fenlands. At Fiskerton Fen Nature Reserve you can see the thriving wetland and reed bed habitats that were largely lost when the area was reclaimed from the marsh. It is home to bitterns, marsh harriers, and to the almost-extinct great water parsnip.

The Water Rail Way is a walking and cycling route that follows the course of the River Witham on the disused Lincoln to Boston railway line. Along the way, you can spot the sculptures inspired by all that is great about Lincolnshire.

27

"Why 'of course'?" Gillian smiled.

"Working dog – she already works the sheep in the holidays and at weekends, and she wants to train her own pup before Gyp gets too old to help."

"Gyp being your dog." Gillian knew that from an exchange back at Christmas when they had had a good chuckle over a slightly risqué card he'd bought for his brother.

The man nodded. His face was kindly, open, without guile.

A horn sounded from outside – sharp imperious blasts.

"Must go. We're on a double yellow," he said with a flash of a smile, showing perfect white teeth. And then, unnecessarily, "And it's farmers' market day, so we've a lot to do."

Gillian felt hard done-by as he left the shop. She looked at the clock. Only six minutes. It was her ambition to keep him for ten.

As it was February, she sold a lot of Valentine's cards that week, and she tried to imagine the recipients of each card from the attitude and style of the purchaser.

She wondered if the farmer would buy one for the imperious horn-blaster on the double yellow lines, and she decided that his wife would be a hard-bitten farming type who would scorn anything as sentimental as a Valentine's card.

Gillian sketched him in charcoal that night. She was pleased with the result: it captured the shy gentleness of him, and the hint of the humour that she knew lay just out of her reach.

She remembered her late husband with a twist. He'd passed away over five years ago, and although she was no longer acutely grieving, she still felt that her heart was on hold.

She'd come down to Devon from London – where, to be honest, she'd never really settled – to make a real go of starting again, but had found herself out of touch with the ways of going out and meeting people. That was why the shop was so good for her.

A WEEK later, at exactly the same time, in walked the sheep farmer, bringing the tang of country air with him.

"Hello." He spoke as soon as he came in this time and Gillian looked up and smiled.

"Valentine?" she guessed.

He looked surprised for a moment and then he smiled his lopsided grin and nodded.

"That's right," he said, and headed for the rack of humorous cards.

Gillian looked at the clock. Right. Ten minutes: go!

She let him look at the stock unhindered for five minutes and then decided to engage him in conversation. If she was really careful, she could spin this out. The blue Land-Rover wasn't outside this morning, so maybe he had a bit more time on his hands. He certainly seemed in no hurry.

He laughed out loud at several of the messages.

"Market day today?" Gillian couldn't think of anything more original to say.

"Every Thursday." He nodded. He then buried his head in the card he was reading, as though he'd said too much.

Gillian looked at the clock again before returning her gaze to the handsome farmer. His hands were clean and there were sparse hairs on the backs of them. She looked surreptitiously at his profile while he was engrossed in the clever joke. He was lean about the jaw line, his hair thick and short, and she wondered what it would feel like under her fingers.

"You should try it," the farmer said.

Gillian flushed scarlet and stepped back slightly.

"The farmers' market," he explained, seeing her high colour and looking puzzled.

"My family specialise in home-reared pork and lamb. You should come and look around. You're not a vegetarian, are you?"

"No," Gillian said, flustered, trying to regain her composure, and then, for something to say, "Do I look like one?"

"No." He tilted his head to one side and looked at her appraisingly. "Outdoor type, though. Good complexion and colour."

That made her blush all the more.

"That's all the walking I do out on the moors." She laughed.

"Yep," he said. "I had you down for a walker, too."

"What do you mean?" It had never occurred to Gillian that he might have been studying her all the time she'd been studying him.

"Great legs." He gave her a broad grin and she blushed so furiously she had to turn away.

"Oh, I'm sorry." One of his big hands touched her arm as lightly as a cat. "No offence intended."

GILLIAN took a deep breath and turned back to him.

"None taken. It's just a bit of a shock when someone turns the tables on you."

"Meaning . . .?"

"I've been trying to visualise all your family, through the cards you buy them. It's a sort of game. I do it for all my customers," she added quickly.

"Can anyone play?" The farmer tipped his head to a couple of other customers, one of whom was approaching the counter with a card from the "humorous" section.

"Go on, then." Gillian smiled at the girl and looked at the card.

It was a birthday card showing a man pulling out a plant from his garden. She turned it over and read the punchline, about the easily pulled plants being the expensive ones, and that was how you knew if you had a weed or not. She chuckled, took the girl's money and popped the card into a bag.

"Well?" Gillian turned to the farmer.

"She's got a dad who's mad on gardening, but isn't very good at it!"

"Good start."

Gillian could see that a card had fallen from one of the shelves and she went over to pick it up, but the farmer had got there first. He lifted it, but didn't hand it back to her.

"So – what did you find out about my family? From my cards, that is?"

"It's a big family, for a start. And you all get on – otherwise you wouldn't buy such nice cards for so many of them. And you've all got a sense of humour, but nothing too rude."

"But that figures for lots of families around here," he said. "Tell me something that only relates to my family."

"They've got a really lovely son, brother, husband, father or uncle!"

"Ah." His tone was suddenly unreadable.

Gillian had an awful sinking feeling, as though she'd not only said the wrong thing, but had spoiled something that might not be reclaimable.

He looked at her and their eyes met.

"Really lovely, you reckon," he repeated slowly after a moment. He held out the card he was holding. "I'll take this one, please."

THEY went back to the counter. Gillian suddenly found she didn't want to be on the other side of it.

"There's no envelope," she floundered.

"Don't need one." He took a pen from his pocket and scribbled on the card and, blushing himself a little now, pushed it over to her. "It's for you. I've got a girl of twelve, two boys of seven and nine, one sister, one brother and two nieces," he confessed. "Plus a mother, father and various cousins. They've had more cards in the past few months than they've ever had. I just kept coming in so that I could see you."

She picked up the card and read: *Please let me take you to dinner tonight – Philip.* Gillian bit her lip.

"What about your wife?"

"Wife? Oh, I'm not married, not any more. Rachel and I . . . we got hitched too young, I suppose. It didn't work out. We still speak, though, and I have the kids every weekend. Sophie's the one with the puppy . . ." He swallowed and his effort to gloss over his situation touched her deeply.

Gillian picked up a card that she knew would make him laugh and wrote in it: *I'd like that very much – Gillian.*

She pushed it back to him and, glancing at the clock, smiled. She'd kept him way beyond the full ten minutes, and it looked as though she would be celebrating her fortieth birthday after all – just a little earlier than anticipated. ■

30

C OTTAGE pie or sausages for supper, Jamie?" Maggie called across the kitchen.

The boy at the scrubbed pine table barely lifted his head from the book he was reading.

"Don't mind," he said unenthusiastically.

"Cottage pie, then," Maggie said. "The beef needs eating up anyway and the sausages can last a bit longer, so we can have them tomorrow."

She was aware of how falsely bright she sounded . . . trying to sound cheerful, trying to keep a smile in her voice.

She looked at the tousled dark head, bent over the book. Small and skinny, the boy perched on the edge of his chair, as if ready to take flight at any moment.

Three months now Jamie had been with them, and they had been a difficult three months. Not because the boy was badly behaved . . . there had been no rudeness, no sullenness, no shouting, arguing or sulks. But he was silent and withdrawn and had raised a barrier between them that Maggie could not breach. She almost felt she would welcome a good old tantrum.

The familiar anger rose in her again at how life had chewed up this little boy. She desperately wanted to go and hug him, but

A Time To Heal

By Tracey Glasspool.

if she did she knew he would stiffen and freeze, and she wasn't sure she could bear that again. She crossed the kitchen and settled for a ruffle of the tousled hair.

"I'll get on with the potatoes," she said. "Could you lay the table, please, Jamie?"

Jamie closed his book, collected the knives and forks and laid them carefully down – a table set for three.

Maggie's thoughts drifted back. The same table, a different time – a table set for two.

"What about adoption?" David had said.

They had been sitting at the kitchen table one Sunday after lunch, he reading and Maggie tackling a crossword.

Maggie had looked up. David's voice had been steady, almost casual, but she had heard the slight catch and seen the tension in his shoulders. She realised he must have been sitting there mustering the courage to say those words.

They talked rarely now about their inability to have children, worn down after years of tests and hoping and disappointment. They had watched as children had been born again and again to friends and family. They loved their nieces and nephews and godchildren, shared in the joy of the new parents, baby-sat, changed nappies, wiped noses and helped with homework. Then they returned to their quiet, peaceful home, just a little bit emptier each time.

✳ ✳ ✳ ✳

Now, at nearly forty, Maggie felt she had made her peace with the situation – accepted that she would not be blessed with motherhood. But she knew that David was less ready to accept a life without children.

He had searched her face and perhaps found some encouragement from what he saw there.

"We could just find out a bit about it," he had continued. "No commitment or anything, just test the waters."

Seeing the hope in his eyes, Maggie had been powerless to argue. She'd agreed, despite her own misgivings and fears, and they had started the process – been vetted and questioned, interviewed and counselled, and all the while in the back of Maggie's mind had been the refrain repeated over and over: what if I can't love a stranger's child?

And then they had met Jamie.

After careful thought they had decided on an older child. Partly because they themselves were older now, partly because combining a busy farm with a demanding baby or toddler would have been too difficult, but mostly because of the stories they heard about older children remaining in care for years, no-one willing to give them a chance.

Jamie had been a perfect example. Abandoned by his mother at five, father unknown, he had been through a succession of foster and care homes before being adopted. Then, to add to his trauma, his adoption had failed. He had been returned like a badly fitting pair of shoes. Since then he had remained in foster care, was now ten years old and had hardened his heart to the world.

As soon as Maggie had met the quiet, gentle boy all her doubts about adoption had disappeared. On the surface he was sensible, mature and self-contained. But behind the brown eyes Maggie had seen a deep well of hurt and bewilderment that she could hardly bear.

A FTER a lengthy period of introductions and outings, Jamie had come to them on a cold January morning. A hoar frost had dusted the farm as if with icing sugar. Shivering from cold and nerves in equal quantities, Maggie and David had ushered Jamie into the warmth of their farmhouse and up to his room.

"I know it looks a little bare at the moment, Jamie, but we thought you would like to choose your own pictures and posters. We can repaint if you don't like the colour, change the curtains – whatever you like. It's your room." Maggie was aware she was babbling.

Jamie had quietly taken in the cream walls, the comfortable bed and the old but solid furniture. He had gone to a bookshelf filled with books and comics and run his fingers over a brand-new box of Lego. Maggie had taken advice from friends with sons of a similar age and kitted the room out accordingly.

She had looked hopefully at him.

"It's fine, thank you," was his cool response, and then he had taken a comic and sat down on the bed to read, withdrawing into his own world again.

That had been three months ago and little had changed since. Jamie remained always polite but distant and aloof. He always answered when spoken to, but rarely initiated any conversation. His social worker told Maggie she was doing all the right things and to give him time. His school teacher said he was quiet at school, but was working hard and seemed content. But Maggie wanted so much more for him – happiness and laughter and joy.

David was coping better. A naturally quiet man, he had taken Jamie on tours of the farm, showing him the barns and the sheep fields. They had walked in companionable silence, David occasionally pointing out and naming trees and birds. He thought Maggie was expecting too much too soon.

When lambing had started Maggie had been relieved to get caught up in the annual chaos. She tried to put worries about Jamie to the back of her mind in the whirl of ewes and lambs.

"Perhaps Jamie would like to help out?" she had said to David, and so the boy had been given little tasks – fetching clean hay and straw, and filling food and water troughs. All of which he had done in his usual quiet, self-sufficient way.

* * * *

With a blast of wind and rain David came clomping into the porch, removing muddy boots before he stepped on to the clean stone floor of the kitchen.

"Got a ewe that won't take to her lamb," he announced. "I've tried all I can but she's not going to feed it. I'll make up a bottle and take it out after supper."

Jamie looked up and David flicked a glance at Maggie at this uncommon spark of interest.

"Want to help, Jamie?" he asked.

Jamie nodded.

After supper they all went to the barn, where a tiny black lamb was lying in the straw. David showed Jamie how to feed the lamb from a bottle and then settled the boy with the lamb in his lap. The lamb suckled for a while and then fell asleep across Jamie's knees.

Maggie caught her breath as, for the first time, a real smile crossed Jamie's face.

Then in a quiet voice he asked, "Can I look after the lamb?"

Maggie and David exchanged looks.

"You can, Jamie," David said, "but it's a long job. He'll have to be fed every four hours day and night, kept warm and dry, and even then there's no guarantee he'll survive."

Jamie nodded.

"I don't mind the work," he said. "It's the school holidays next week and I promise I won't miss a single feed."

It was the longest sentence Maggie had heard from him.

JAMIE was true to his word. Maggie or David took him down to the barn each time, busy with their own jobs but able to keep an eye on him. And as Jamie cared for the lamb he slowly began to emerge from his silent world. He started to make little comments, almost to himself at first, about the lamb and the other sheep in the barn. Then gradually he began to ask questions directly, about other work on the farm. Maggie answered his questions calmly and carefully, trying to contain the hope rising in her.

The lamb was tiny and weak, and although he took milk he barely moved. Maggie heard Jamie coaxing and whispering to him as he offered the bottle, warming the little body with his hands. She willed the lamb to survive, realising that a link had been made to the troubled boy through the tiny scrap.

Then, one morning, Maggie and Jamie opened the barn door to see the lamb

34

Fifty Years Ago . . .

March 10, 1964

To many it must seem like just yesterday and not 50 years ago that the Queen was delivered of her fourth child, the baby of the family, Prince Edward Antony Richard Louis.

Like his brothers before him, Prince Edward attended Gordonstoun before working as a tutor in New Zealand during his gap year. Following his graduation from Cambridge University, and a short spell in the Royal Marines, he worked in the theatre and television. A documentary on his great-uncle, Edward VIII, was particularly well received.

On his marriage to Sophie Rhys-Jones, Edward was given the title Earl of Essex with the Palace announcing that in time he would succeed to the title Duke of Edinburgh, making it appropriate that he took over his father's role in the Duke of Edinburgh Award Scheme and as president of the Commonwealth Games Federation.

Away from the spotlight, he and his wife enjoy family life with their children, Lady Louise Windsor and James, Viscount Severn. ∎

on his feet, wobbling on the straw. The lamb bleated pitifully when it saw Jamie and then tottered and stumbled straight to him and pressed its soft nose into his hand. Jamie looked up at Maggie with such a look of delight on his face that it stopped her heart. She saw David passing by outside and called quietly to him.

Jamie stood looking at the lamb for a while, caressing its nose.

"It's not fair, is it – that his mum didn't want him?" he said.

Maggie pressed her lips together, willing the tears not to fall.

"No, love," she said softly. "It's not fair at all."

"Why does that happen?" Jamie's voice was no more than a whisper.

"Nobody really knows. Some sheep just aren't made for mothering." Maggie stopped then, unable to continue.

David squeezed her shoulder and carried on, choosing his words with care.

"Sometimes a mum's too young and doesn't know what to do," he said, "or perhaps she's poorly. Or sometimes they simply can't cope."

Jamie stood silently for a minute more, the lamb snuffling him, searching for the bottle.

Then to Maggie's surprise and joy she felt a small, warm hand pressed into her own.

"But this lamb will be all right, won't he?" Jamie whispered. "Because he's got us."

Us, Maggie thought. She had never heard a more beautiful word. She squeezed the small hand in hers tightly.

"Yes, Jamie, love," she said. "He'll be fine. He'll always have us." ■

Do The Worst First

I ALWAYS put off certain jobs
I know I should do now,
But I've decided that from today
I'll do them all somehow.

As leaving them I quite forget
Until it's far too late,
For if, like me, the job done last
Is always one I hate.

So I've resolved that I'll do first
The tasks put off the most,
Then cheerfully if someone asks,
"I've done them!" I can boast.

– *Chrissy Greenslade.*

Thinkstockphotos.

My Crowning Glory!

Illustration by Maggie Palmer.

IT'S an odd thing about handicrafts, either you love doing them or you hate them. A bit like Marmite, you either love it or hate it, there's no middle ground.

So when the committee of the over-fifties club announced that we'd be having an Easter bonnet competition, half the members groaned and the other half immediately lit up. You'll probably be able to guess which group I belong to.

I was never very good with a needle, or wool, or glue. Luckily, my big sister, Fran, had a real gift for arts and crafts and managed to rescue me from many of my messes. She'd unpicked the sleeve from a blouse I'd tried to make at school and sewn it on the right way round. She'd helped me with my school projects and knitted matinée coats and booties for both my children.

I just thanked my lucky stars that my daughter, Marina, had inherited all

—————— **by Christine Evans.** —————— 37

her skills. I'd put off the pesky Easter bonnet-making until the last moment. My friends at the club were full of ideas and always chatting away about their projects.

"What are you doing, Rita?" May asked.

"Oh, it's still at the planning stage," I muttered.

"Right!" Fran commented with a chuckle. She'd been widowed like me recently and come to live nearby. She'd joined the club when I'd told her what fun it was and it was lovely to have her there.

"Would you like any help?"

"No, of course not," I protested. "I can manage."

What was I talking about? Of course I couldn't!

I desperately needed help and my plan was to rope Marina in.

Unfortunately, she came bouncing into the house with plans of her own.

"Oh, Mum, I've got great news! Gerry has booked us a surprise holiday in Paris for Easter week. It was a cancellation he spotted on the internet and it's so cheap."

"That's lovely," I said, my heart sinking.

"The thing is, I don't suppose you could mind Buster for me? We can't really afford to put him in kennels for a week because they're so expensive, and you know what he's like . . ."

"Of course, love. I can manage Buster."

"Are you sure?" she asked anxiously.

Buster was a boisterous mongrel. My daughter and Gerry hadn't started a family yet and he was their baby. Of course, you don't earn a name like Buster by being a meek little pooch.

WOULD you have time to help me make an Easter bonnet before you go?" I asked.

Marina's face fell.

"Oh, Mum, I don't think I will. Gerry's rather sprung this holiday on me and I've got a heap of washing and ironing to do before we go. And I promised Mr Cane at work that I'd work late a couple of evenings so I could have the extra time off."

"Oh, dear."

She must have guessed my disappointment because she immediately started firing ideas at me while she made us a cup of tea.

"What do you like doing best?" she asked.

"Gardening," I said without hesitation.

Now that was something I was good at. I'm proud to say my garden was a picture. In fact, I'd provided most of the over-fifties club members with cuttings and was always getting them coming to me for tips. I was pleased to help, especially when I knew I could dig out my late husband's ancient and much-thumbed notebook when I got stuck.

"Why not do a gardening hat?" she suggested. "You've still got that old straw sun hat that you brought back from Spain, haven't you? Why not stick some silk flowers on it and that butterfly brooch? If you really wanted to go the whole hog, you could even add that plastic robin you have for the Christmas tree."

"And I've got that little plastic leprechaun you brought me back from Ireland that could do as a garden gnome," I said, suddenly inspired.

Not that I was keen on garden gnomes. But now I could actually see the hat in my mind's eye. It would be magnificent. Even my sister would have to be impressed by it!

I drove Gerry and Marina to the airport and came home to find Buster ripping apart one of his soft toys.

"Oh, you are a mess pot," I scolded mildly, clearing up the debris.

He gave me one of those looks that is probably just panting, but looks to me like a cheeky grin. Gerry had assured me that he'd had a good walk that morning, so I decided to assemble all my bits and pieces and finally started the hat.

The butterfly brooch was easy – it just pinned on the straw. I raided the flower arrangement in the hall and tried some long stitches to attach the roses. They just wouldn't lie straight, however, so I had to add a few more stitches. There were more stitches than I'd intended now and they looked very untidy.

I was inspired to snip a strand of ivy from another arrangement and draped it round to hide the stitches. The robin from my Christmas decorations perched nicely on top – with the wires on his feet pushed through the straw and twisted underneath. I can't tell you how satisfied I felt. Perhaps there was something in this handicrafts lark, after all.

The leprechaun, however, proved tricky.

"Call yourself lucky!" I scolded the little grinning figure as I picked him up from the floor yet again. Buster sniffed at him and grinned, too. "Oh, don't look at me like that. I know I'm talking to leprechauns now!"

Not to mention talking to a dog.

FINALLY, I tied the little figure steady with another strand of ivy. He was a bit wobbly, but at least he was attached. I tried on the hat. In the mirror I looked a bit like Worzel Gummidge, but I have to say the hat was a triumph. I was quietly confident that I would impress the judges, not to mention my sister. Just one more day to go and I was sure of a prize for my Easter bonnet.

The next day was busy. I took Buster for a long walk – or rather he took me – and we ended up at Fran's bungalow. He licked her lavishly and she gave him a biscuit.

"So this is Buster? He looks like a lively mutt," she said, laughing. "Have

Forecast, Light Winds

SWEEPING from the wings again,
"Just me," new March declares,
As wind whistles at the windows
And rattles 'neath the stairs.
It blows high in the rafters,
Comes howling at the door,
It makes the shutters shiver
And creaks the parquet floor.
Why does March cause such a stir
When springtime sits serene?
Perhaps she's just the wild child –
A breeze on nature's scene!

– Dorothy McGregor.

you had time to make your hat yet?"

"I have," I said proudly. "It's all finished and ready to go."

My sister gave me a very searching look.

"Finished? What's it like?"

"It's a secret. Anyway, you'll see it tomorrow."

I could see she was wondering if my creation would actually appear and what it would look like without my regular helpers.

I CHOSE a floral dress to go with my hat and I have to say it looked very nice. The weather wasn't brilliant, so I decided to put on a cardigan that I could remove later on. I nipped upstairs to get the cardigan from my bedroom and left my hat on the chair in the hall.

Buster was grinning when I returned. In fact, he looked very pleased with himself. He'd managed to chew the leprechaun from the hat and in the process had demolished the roses. Half the brim was chewed off and my creation was a wreck.

I was so angry that I roared at him. He quickly retreated behind the settee as I surveyed my ruined hat. I could have cried.

Palm House, Belfast

THE Palm House is situated near Queen's University Belfast in the Botanic Gardens. Designed by Charles Lanyon, the Palm House is one of the earliest examples of a curvilinear cast-iron glasshouse. Its construction was initiated by the Belfast Botanical and Horticultural Society in the 1830s.

The two wings were completed in 1840, and were built by Richard Turner of Dublin, who later built the Great Palm House at Kew Gardens. Over the years, the Palm House has acquired a reputation for good plant collections. The cool wing houses all-year-round displays of colour and scent using plants such as geranium, fuchsia, begonia and built displays.

The Tropical Ravine, or Fernery, completed in 1889, is a fine example of horticultural Victoriana. The plants grow in a sunken glen overlooked by a balcony. The stove wing and dome area contain a range of temperate and tropical plants with particular emphasis on species of economic value.

Checking the time on my watch, I realised that I had ten minutes to try to put things right. I half-heartedly tied the leprechaun back on with the ivy and it dangled limply. The robin's beak was bent and some of his tail feathers missing. I tried to revive the roses and trimmed the chewed brim as best I could with scissors. Sticking my hat in a carrier bag, I went with a sinking heart to the over-fifties club.

At least I could show them I'd made the effort, I reasoned.

Everyone else was buzzing with excitement. And I have to say that there were some spectacular bonnets on display.

"Where's your Easter bonnet, then?" Fran asked, a magnificent creation like a wedding cake perched on her head.

"The dog ate it," I said dejectedly.

She began to giggle, then roared with laughter. My sister's laugh has always been infectious and others joined in, too.

"The dog ate it," she gasped, tears rolling down her face. "I've heard some excuses, Rita, but that takes the biscuit."

So much for the sympathy, then!

"No, honestly," I said, taking the poor crumpled effort from the carrier bag. "I only left it for a couple of minutes to go upstairs for a cardigan and Buster demolished it."

"It's not so bad," May said. "Put it on. You could go as the wreck of the *Hesperus*!"

That set them all off laughing again.

"It could be a scene from a wild garden," someone else suggested more helpfully.

"My garden looks like that anyway," another member pointed out.

I DONNED my creation, all pride in my handicrafts efforts as battered as the hat. But would you believe that I won a prize? They gave me one because my hat had the best story attached to it.

Everyone else's hats were merely designs, but I explained about my love of gardening and how the dog had made my lovely gardening hat into a wild garden. The judges nodded in approval and gave me a prize. To be honest, it was probably a sympathy vote, but I enjoyed the chocolates all the same.

"At least you won a prize," Fran commented as we walked home. "You upheld the family honour."

The winner had been a volcano hat with puffs of smoke coming from the crater. It was provided by one of those air fresheners that puffs out spray now and again and looked most effective.

"My grandson did help me," the winner had admitted as she accepted the bouquet of flowers.

Well, I'm proud to say that at least my Easter bonnet was all my own work, even if it did end up looking like the dog's dinner! ■

First Steps

by
Kate Jackson.

I **THOUGHT** Eve could do it." Hearing my name, I looked up from the computer screen where I was trying to find a book for Mr Thomas, one of our regulars, who vaguely remembered the name of the author but wasn't sure. It was proving to be quite a search.

"I didn't catch that," I said to my boss, Stella, who was smiling broadly at me, her arms full of books ready to go back on the reshelving trolley.

"I was just saying to Carrie that I thought you'd do a good job taking over the Toddlers' Story Time next week. Don't you think so?"

"Me?" I stared at Stella and then shifted my gaze to Carrie, my other colleague, who raised her eyebrows at me.

"Yes. I think you'll be perfect. It'll give you more experience and besides," Stella said with a grin, "one of us has got to do it." Before I had a chance to say anything she loaded the books on

43

to the reshelving trolley and steered it off in the direction of Fiction, leaving me staring after her.

Toddlers' Story Time, I thought. Me, read to the group of little people who came in every Tuesday morning, rain or shine, along with their parents, grandparents or childminders, and sat themselves down on the brightly coloured rug in the children's section, ready for the songs and stories that Carrie so expertly read and sang to them. Or she did until this morning.

She had just led her last Toddlers' Story Time before she left on her round-the-world trip. She would be gone for six whole months.

"It's fun. Honestly," Carrie tried to reassure me. "And I'm sure you can do it. I've a song book I use and . . ."

Mr Thomas cleared his throat and looked at me sympathetically.

"Sorry, Eve, but I must get the twelve o'clock bus . . ."

"Of course. Sorry, Mr Thomas."

"I'll talk to you about it later," Carrie said.

I smiled gratefully at her and resumed my search for Mr Thomas's mystery book, with the worry of being in charge of Toddlers' Story Time hovering over me like a heavy, black cloud.

I never managed to talk to Carrie, as it turned out to be one of those days when we were constantly busy with one thing or another, and by the time we closed it was too late. Carrie's husband picked her up from work and I waved them off at the door. They were returning home briefly and then heading straight for the airport. It was only when I collected my bag from my locker in the staff room that I found a sheet of paper tucked into the sliver of a gap around the door. I pulled it out and recognised Carrie's writing.

Dear Eve, it said. *Don't worry about doing Toddlers' Story Time. I was nervous about it when I started. Remember children love having stories read to them, so just try to bring the story to life. Put on voices for the characters and point things out in the pictures. Perhaps if you practised reading to some children beforehand, it would help you to feel more confident.*

Enjoy it, Eve, it's good fun and, who knows, you might not want to stop when I come back!

Love, Carrie.

I didn't think Carrie's final point was likely to happen. I didn't even want to start, but it would have seemed churlish of me not to at least give it a try. If I followed Carrie's advice and got some practice in first, then at least I would be a bit more experienced when facing a sea of expectant toddlers the following Tuesday morning.

But the question was, how and where was I going to get some practice?

I didn't have any children of my own, but if I did, I wouldn't have had this problem, as I'd already be used to reading to them, I reckoned. So I had to find a way to get some experience beforehand. Like learning all new things I should take it slowly, step by step. Perhaps read to just one child to start with. And I suddenly knew who my first audience could be. William.

A S soon as I got home I rang my best friend, Sandra, William's mother, and explained my problem, and Sandra being Sandra, she was more than happy to help. So it was arranged for me to go and practise reading to William on Wednesday afternoon, my half day at the library.

William was my godson, and I saw him often, but I must confess that I'd never actually read a story to him. Sandra was always reading to him and William had developed a deep love of books. So I never felt I should read to him when I visited. I loved getting down on the floor and playing trains with him, building up his lovely wooden train track, putting in bridges and tunnels. Reading to him would be a new experience altogether. For both of us.

I arrived on Sandra's doorstep on a Wednesday afternoon, armed with a bag of picture books which I'd carefully selected from the children's section in the library. They were ones which I thought might be good to read in Toddlers' Story Time and I wanted to try them out on William first.

As soon as Sandra opened the door with William in her arms, he gave me a big smile and wriggled to be put down.

"Hello, William," I said, crouching down and loving the warm feeling inside as he threw his arms around me.

"Hello, Eve!" William grabbed my hand and pulled me over the doorstep and towards the sitting-room. "Come play trains."

Sandra caught my eye and laughed.

"It looks like reading is going to have to compete with playing trains."

I hadn't thought William would think like that. I'd been so wrapped up in worrying about Toddlers' Story Time, I hadn't taken into account that William would think we'd play like we always did. Reading instead of playing trains might take a bit of persuading.

But Sandra quickly put her experience of living with a toddler into practice.

"William," she said, "Eve needs your help. She has to read to some children in the library where she works, and she doesn't know which books they'd like, so do you think you could help her choose them before you play trains today?"

William looked up at me from where he'd started to empty the large box of wooden train track on to the carpet, and for a moment I thought he was going to say no.

"I've brought lots of books to choose from." I took them out of my bag. "Which ones do you think I should read next week?"

To my relief William stood up and came over to look at the colourful books. Before I knew it we had both settled down in the big armchair by the window, William snuggled up on my lap with the first book he'd chosen for me to read.

Reading to William felt wonderful. I found myself relaxing into it, putting on voices for the characters as Carrie had suggested, and together we looked at the pictures carefully, pointing things out to each other. It felt like the most natural thing in the world and I began to think that my jitters about Toddlers' Story Time had been ill founded.

But then a little voice whispered in my mind that the set-up in the library, warm, welcoming and child-friendly as it was, wasn't the same as sitting one-to-one with a child you've known and loved since birth. I quickly quelled the thought, determined to think positively. I knew that reading to William wasn't the same, but it was surely a step in the right direction.

WE were so engrossed in the next book that I didn't notice visitors had arrived until I heard voices in the hall. I looked up and saw three other little people dashing into the sitting-room, and Sandra and another woman I hadn't met before followed in behind.

Sandra quickly introduced us all and somehow, the three other children – two girls and a boy who were a similar age to William – settled themselves down on the rug in front of my chair and looked expectantly up at me as if they wanted to join in with the story.

Suddenly my audience of one child snuggled up on my lap became four. I glanced over at Sandra, who shrugged her shoulders and grinned back at me.

"Why don't you try out some of the other books, Eve?" she said. "See which ones prove popular?"

I had the feeling that this was meant to happen. That Sandra had arranged for her friend to drop in with her triplets, to provide more of a challenge for me.

"William, I'm going to need to hold the book in a different way so everyone can see the pictures," I explained, thinking of how I'd seen Carrie do it. "So could you please sit down on the rug with the others?"

He happily obliged and I took a deep breath, opened the first page of the book and began to read.

＊　＊　＊　＊

I was nervous when Tuesday morning arrived. I had checked and rechecked that everything was ready for the children's arrival. The colourful cushions were scattered around the rug to make comfy seats. I had my books to hand and I'd practised reading them so often I virtually knew them off by heart.

My experience reading to William and his friends had left me feeling quietly optimistic. They had been a lovely audience, who'd joined in with the repetitive bits in one of the stories and who'd laughed at my funny voices. So as the first of the toddlers began to arrive, I did my best to calm my nerves and feel confident.

But my optimism rapidly dissolved, when my presence in what they regarded as Carrie's armchair clearly didn't meet with the approval of several children. When I explained to them that Carrie wasn't here, two children suddenly burst into noisy sobs. I had to think fast.

In desperation I reached up for the globe on top of one of the book shelves and settled myself back in the armchair.

"Does anyone know what this is?" I asked.

"A ball," one little girl offered.

"It's a ball shape," I said. "It's a model of something."

I explained that it was a model of the world and all the different countries were shown on it. I told them about Carrie's trip around the world and that she had promised to send postcards to us.

"Every time we get a postcard from her," I told them, "we'll look on the globe to see where she is. We'll be able to follow her travels around the world."

I was relieved that by the time we finished talking about Carrie's trip, the sobbing children had calmed down and were staring at me, wide eyed, from the security of their parents' laps.

While they were quiet I grabbed my first book and hesitantly began to read.

AFTER the rocky start, my first Toddlers' Story Time flew past. All the tales seemed to go down well, and my different voices for each character helped to bring the stories alive. I was both relieved and delighted when many of the children and their parents came to thank me at the end. Even the two children who had cried managed to smile at me and waved goodbye when they left.

"You did an excellent job," Stella said, handing me a cup of coffee in the staff room later on. "Did you enjoy it?"

"I did, actually. After they stopped crying."

"They'll probably cry when Carrie comes back. Some children like the same routine and anything or anyone different upsets them." Stella took a sip of her coffee and looked at me.

"You know, perhaps we should think about you and Carrie sharing the running of Toddlers' Story Time when she gets back."

"Maybe," I replied, though I was surprised to find myself even considering it.

I had six months' worth of Toddlers' Story Times to make up my mind. I would take it step by step, and if nobody cried when they saw it was me sitting in the armchair next week, then I'd know I was getting somewhere. ■

Recipe For Love

SALLY CLOUGH popped an extra teaspoon of paprika into the casserole she was gently agitating on the stove. She was trying a Middle Eastern recipe from a new cookery book she had got from the library. The list of ingredients was long and mostly unobtainable in her local shops so she was improvising. She added some dried chillies and extra lemon juice, hoping they would be a suitable substitute for the elusive sumac powder, and tasted the liquid in the pan.

Very spicy, very Middle Eastern, she thought, ignoring the sour taste at the back of her throat. There was a picture in the cookery book of a spice market in Lebanon. Sally tried to imagine how it would smell, with all those exotic aromas mingling in the heat. She would have loved to visit some of the places in her books but Ben was not keen. He didn't like the heat and was nervous of strange beds and food, so Sally contented herself with travelling the world from her kitchen. The recipes were not always a complete success and she knew that Ben would have preferred a nice shepherd's pie, but the cooking eased her wanderlust and made her feel modern and adventurous.

She was adding a dash of tabasco to the casserole when the back door opened and her husband came in, holding a large bunch of rhubarb.

"George gave me this for borrowing my drill," he told her. "I was thinking maybe a nice crumble?"

"Oh, no." Sally seized the rhubarb with delight. "I've a Keralan recipe I've been wanting to try for ages. You bake it with Earl Grey tea and cardamom pods and serve it with clove-infused custard."

Ben tried hard to disguise his disappointment. He liked his custard plain and un-infused. But Sally was so modern in her outlook that he was afraid she saw him as just an old stick in the mud, so when she embarked on a culinary journey around the world, he ate whatever she cooked without complaint.

"Is this for tea?" he asked, indicating the casserole.

"Yes," Sally replied. "It's called lamb harrah. It's Lebanese. I just need to add these." She reached for a jar of preserved lemons which her son had brought her from London by special request. Ben sniffed cautiously at the pan.

"I was thinking we might go to the steak night at the pub tomorrow," he ventured.

"Oh, no, Ben," Sally replied. "I'm doing bouillabaisse tomorrow."

The preserved lemons gave off a vague smell of toilet cleaner as she chopped them, and Ben thought wistfully of the food Sally used to cook;

by Jenny Hays.

stews and broth and pies – the food they and their children had grown up with, but which Sally now saw as hopelessly outdated.

"So what about lunch?" he asked briskly, afraid Sally might sense his nostalgia and take it as a rebuke. "Shall I have some bread and cheese?"

"No, no." Sally waved him away from the bread bin. "The children are coming – I'll make some fajitas with guacamole and hummus, and I've got a pineapple for afters with cashew cream."

"Will they like that?" Ben asked doubtfully.

"Of course," Sally replied. "They eat that sort of thing all the time and it's very healthy. You know how Sarah fusses over their five a day."

Ben did know and, in his opinion, if his grandchildren were fed proper food instead of pizzas, fajitas and anything else ending in an "a", their intake of fruit and vegetables would take care of itself.

A S Sally put the lid on the casserole the door burst open and Alice, the eldest of their grandchildren, bounced into the kitchen closely followed by her younger sister, Maisie, and her brother, Tom. Alice was holding a clipboard.

"We're doing a project on healthy eating at school," she announced. "I need to know what you used to eat in the olden days."

"The olden days," Sally said brightly, immediately feeling about a hundred years old. "Well, that was a long time ago. What did we used to eat, Grandad? Can you remember that far back?"

"I remember we didn't have any fajitas or harrahs," Ben replied, "and we ate a lot of bread, with cheese."

Sally pulled a face at him and thought hard. She was so intent on finding new recipes that she hardly ever gave any thought to the meals of her childhood.

"We ate a lot of stews, I suppose," she said. "And broth with dumplings. And pies and puddings." She smiled at Alice. "In fact, all the things your mummy doesn't like you to have." She felt Ben harrumph beside her.

Alice consulted her clipboard.

"Did you have five portions of fruit and vegetables a day?" she asked.

"We didn't know we were supposed to." Sally laughed. "My dad grew lots of vegetables, so I expect we did."

She was surprised by a sudden memory of sitting on the step with her sister, topping and tailing gooseberries. She wondered briefly if the children had even tasted a gooseberry.

"I ate a lot of carrots," Ben said. "That's why I can see round corners."

Maisie hugged his legs.

"Grandad, you are funny," she said.

Tom peered at the clipboard over his sister's shoulder.

"What was your favourite food?" he asked his gran.

Sally watched Alice painstakingly spelling broth and dumplings and unexpectedly recalled the delight of running into the house on a cold day to be greeted by soup simmering on the stove and the smell of newly baked bread.

She thought of the cheese and onion pie that had been her father's favourite, and the pickled red cabbage her grandma made to accompany it. She pictured the steamy kitchen of her childhood with the washing drying on the rack and her mother rolling pastry, her cheeks flushed from the heat and flecked with flour, and she smiled. There was always some left-over pastry from the pie, and her mother had made it into very special little pasties for lunch the next day.

"Well," she said, "I think my favourite food in the world was butter pie."

"Butter pie," Alice repeated, appalled. "You can't make a pie full of butter."

"No, of course you can't," Sally agreed. "It wasn't a pie full of butter. It was a pie full of potato with a big blob of butter in the middle."

"It sounds delicious," Maisie said.

"It doesn't sound like healthy eating," Alice said doubtfully, chewing the end of her pencil.

"Butter pies made me the man I am today," Ben said, puffing out his stomach and patting it proudly. Alice looked even more sceptical, but Sally smiled at her husband. How could she have forgotten about butter pies?

She lifted the lid of the casserole bubbling on the stove to give it a stir and Maisie wrinkled her nose.

"That smells funny," she said. "Did you eat that when you were little?"

"No," Sally replied.

"No," Ben said emphatically.

"We didn't really eat anything foreign," Sally explained.

"What's foreign?" Maisie asked.

"From other countries," Ben explained. "Like spaghetti from Italy and chow mein from China."

"And paella from Spain, and curry from Asia and hummus from Greece," Sally said. "No-one knew anything about those foods when we were little. It was only when people started to go abroad for their holidays that we began to learn about such things."

BEN felt the guilt wash over him again. He loved his wife, he loved the home they had made together and he saw no reason to leave it. They took their holidays in their caravan, taking their home with them, and Ben felt that this was the only way to travel. However, he knew that Sally yearned to explore the world and he wished he could be the adventurous companion she deserved.

"I remember the first time I ate spaghetti," he said quickly, to show that he wasn't a complete dinosaur.

"My auntie Joan liked to try new recipes – just like your granny does – and when she put a plate of spaghetti bolognese in front of my dad, do you know what he said?"

Maisie shook her head.

"He said, 'What's this, Joan? Have you boiled up your knitting?'"

The children all shrieked with laughter and Sally joined in.

"Your grandad takes after his dad," she said. "He doesn't really like foreign food, either."

"Don't you, Grandad?" Maisie asked.

"I like everything your granny cooks," Ben said firmly.

"Oh, Ben." Sally shook her head laughingly at him. "You know you'd rather have shepherd's pie than lamb harrah."

"I like everything your granny cooks," Ben repeated, "because she always puts a special ingredient in."

"Salt," Maisie suggested.

"Chillies," Tom shouted. He who had eaten many of his granny's curries.

"Preserved lemons?" Sally suggested, laughing.

Ben smiled and shook his head. He was about to speak when Tom interrupted him.

"Granny," he said, "can we have butter pie for lunch?"

"Well." Sally looked doubtfully at the avocados on the counter. "I was going to make fajitas."

"Butter pie! Butter pie!" Maisie began to chant and soon Tom and Alice joined in, too.

"I think you're out-voted, Sally," Ben said. "Just make sure you make one for me," he told Maisie.

"Do you like butter pies, too?" she asked.

Ben looked at his wife and raised his eyebrows.

"Do I like butter pie?" he asked her.

SALLY smiled at him with her very special smile that told him he was still the only man for her, even if he was a boring old stick in the mud. "Your grandad liked butter pies so much he used to swap me his 'Beano' for one every week," she told her grandchildren. She smiled her special smile at him again. "And he hasn't had a butter pie for years, so let's push the boat out and make him one," she said.

"What does 'push the boat out' mean?" Alice asked.

"Oh, it just means to do something special," Sally answered. "I don't really know why we say it, Ben, do you?"

Ben shook his head thoughtfully.

"Pushing the boat out," he said slowly. "I think it's about being generous and doing something special for someone else."

He seemed to be deep in thought for a moment but then he grinned.

Fifty Years Ago . . . April 20, 1964

MANY will remember when we all sat around our black and white television sets to await the launch of Britain's third TV channel – BBC2. However, fate stepped in and a huge power failure, originating from a fire at Battersea Power Station, caused Television Centre to lose all power, forcing the BBC to postpone the launch. As a result "Play School" was the first programme to be shown officially on the channel. The launch schedule of "light entertainment" was rescheduled for the following evening. The transmission opened with a shot of a lit candle which was blown out by presenter Denis Tuohy – cutting-edge humour for the BBC of the Sixties.

Three years later around six million viewers tuned in on Sunday evenings to watch the memorable series "The Forsyte Saga", adapted from the novels of John Galsworthy with a cast that included Kenneth More, Eric Porter and Nyree Dawn Porter.

As well as giving a platform to quality drama and entertainment, BBC2 also gave over a considerable amount of air time to the Open University, helping to make education more readily available.

All photography © BBC.

53

"Like making someone a butter pie, while he has a quiet moment in his shed."

The children had a hilarious time helping Sally to make the pies. Tom stuck bits of pastry to his chin to create a moustache and Alice carved faces into the potatoes. Maisie was entrusted with the vital task of adding a generous blob of butter to the pies, and ended up with quite a lot on the end of her nose.

When the pies were ready for the oven Alice consulted her clipboard yet again.

"Did you have take-aways?" she asked.

"Well, I suppose we did," Sally admitted, "but we didn't call them that. Dad got paid on Fridays, so he always got fish and chips on his way home." Once again she was hijacked by a vivid memory of running down the road to meet her smiling father, and then running back up the hill with the moist and fragrant paper parcels in her hands.

"Fish and chips from a chip shop?" Tom asked in wonder.

"With no vegetables?" Alice asked in equal wonder. Sally could see in her eyes that she really did not understand how her grandmother had managed to survive so long without her five a day.

The pies began to fill the kitchen with a delicious buttery aroma and the children helped Sally to set the table.

JUST as they finished, the door opened and Sally's son, Daniel, walked in. "What a delicious smell," he said appreciatively. "It smells like the old days, Mum."

"Daddy," Maisie squealed, "we're having butter pies."

"Really?" Daniel looked questioningly at his mother.

"Yes, really," she replied.

"Have you ever had butter pie?" Alice asked.

"Oh, yes," her father replied. "My granny used to make them for me every week."

Tom turned towards his grandmother.

"You've never made butter pies for us," he said accusingly.

"Well," Sally defended herself, "I've made you lots of other things, like clam chowder and enchiladas and spaghetti Milanese."

"Huh," Maisie said, "that's just boiled knitting."

Daniel looked confused.

"We've just been talking about food from the olden days," Sally told him. "That's why we're making butter pies instead of fajitas."

"Well, I'm glad," Daniel said. He admired his mother's modern outlook but missed the comforting food of his childhood. "You never make good old-fashioned food any more. I used to love your cheese and onion pie, and broth and dumplings and jam roly poly."

"Roly poly, roly poly," Maisie chanted.

"But they're not really healthy, are they?" Sally protested.

"Well, we seem to have done all right on them." Her son laughed. "And I used to love the stories. Granny had a story to tell about everything she made. That's what grannies do, Mum. They keep history alive for the next generation."

Sally felt stricken. Was she failing in her duty as a granny? Daniel laughed at her crestfallen expression.

"Don't worry, Mum," he said. "I'm glad you're a modern granny, but I'm also glad you still remember how to make butter pies."

"The pies!" Sally said, jumping up from the sofa and pulling them from the oven just in time. As she did so, Ben walked into the kitchen.

"Butter pies," he said enthusiastically. "Just like the old days, eh, Dan?"

SALLY bit into the crisp pastry and the warm buttery potato and looked at Ben over the crust. Butter was dripping down his chin and his eyes met hers. Sally was immediately transported back to her childhood.

Every week she had taken her butter pie to his cottage next door to the school and silently exchanged her pie for his copy of the "Beano". His parents both worked so they could afford comics but had no time for baking. It was a perfect solution. Sally wasn't thinking about France or the Middle East or Mexico; she was back in her childhood with the boy she loved. She smiled around the table at her husband, her son and her grandchildren as they tucked into the pies with appreciative murmurs.

How foolish she was, Sally thought, fretting about foreign travel when she had everything she needed right here.

That afternoon Ben announced that he was off to the DIY store and Daniel took Tom to football practice, dropping the girls off at ballet on the way. Sally tidied the kitchen and inspected the lamb harrah.

She thought about what Daniel had said. She'd been trying so hard to be a modern granny that she had forgotten that grannies should help to keep the past alive. The children often asked her about "the olden days", but she preferred to talk to them about what was happening at school, or with their friends, so that she could keep up to date. It was Ben who told them about making dens in the woods and dams in streams and Saturday morning pictures.

Ben, her lovely Ben, who loved her so much that he was prepared to eat bouillabaisse and lamb harrah without complaint. So many of their childhood memories involved food – picnics, school outings, days out on their bikes, and always with a slab of home-made pie and cake to keep them company. Why had she turned her back on all those lovely memories?

You could look backwards as well as forwards, she thought. You could treasure old-fashioned things as well as modern ones.

That evening, when Ben opened the door he was greeted by an unexpected but strangely familiar smell. He glanced around the kitchen – there was no hint of what it might be, no recipe books on the counter, no jars of strange spices.

Sally was stirring a pan at the stove and turned to greet him. He put the large envelope he had been holding on to the table and moved towards her. He looked into the pan.

"Is that . . ." he hesitated for a moment ". . . custard?"

"Yes," Sally replied with a smile.

"Infused with something?" Ben ventured.

"No," Sally answered. "Just plain simple yellow custard, and I've made a rhubarb crumble to put it on."

Ben rubbed his hands together in anticipation.

"Rhubarb crumble," he said delightedly. "I didn't think I'd eat that again."

"I know," Sally replied, "but today I realised that all those foods I call old-fashioned are an important part of us. They bring back such happy memories."

Ben put her arms around her.

"I know just what you mean," he told her. "But you know I'll eat anything you make for me because of that special ingredient."

Sally looked at him quizzically.

"I put so many ingredients in," she said. "I didn't know you had a favourite spice."

Ben shook his head.

"I don't," he said. "Your special ingredient is love. You always put love into your cooking, Sally. Love for me, love for your family and love of life, so no matter how many spices or . . ." he gave a little grimace ". . . preserved lemons you put in, I can always taste the love."

SALLY looked at him and felt her eyes fill with tears. She had cooked for Ben all their married life and he had always been appreciative, but she'd had no idea he thought so deeply about it. She thought guiltily about the rhubarb he had brought and the way he'd generously tried to hide his disappointment at her plans for it.

"Oh, Ben," she said, hugging him hard. "You must love me very much to eat some of the meals I've made for you."

"I do," Ben replied, kissing the top of her head. "Now, when will that lamb haha be ready?"

"Harrah," Sally said, flapping him with her tea towel. "But we're not having it."

Ben raised his eyebrows questioningly.

"Those preserved lemons tasted like toilet cleaner," she told him. "It's in the bin." Ben suppressed a smile and Sally continued. "I've decided that as well as travelling the world, we should travel back in time. So tonight, Ben, we're having shepherd's pie. Can you guess why?"

"Moving into our first house," Ben replied promptly. "Sitting on a tea chest eating your mum's shepherd's pie straight out of the dish with spoons. It was so cold we were wrapped together in a blanket while we ate."

"That's right," Sally said delightedly. "And the next day we couldn't face the unpacking so we went on a winter picnic instead."

"With your mum's famous sausage plait," Ben said. "Do you remember that time the bull chased us out of the field but I went back for it?"

"And the cows had trampled it." Sally smiled.

"What a tragedy." Ben shook his head sadly and then looked slyly at Sally. "I wonder if I'll ever eat a sausage plait again?"

"Sausage plait, cheese and onion pie, gingerbread – anything you like," Sally said. "I need to start making all those old recipes again so I don't forget how to."

"My mouth is watering already," Ben told her. "How long will the pie be?"

"Another ten minutes," Sally replied. "The potatoes just need to brown."

"Then sit down," Ben said. "Tell me what you think of this."

HE picked up the envelope and pulled out the contents. Sally stared.
"A cruise?"

"A cruise," Ben agreed. "A culinary cruise of the Mediterranean. You visit different countries and sample eleven different cuisines, but you don't need to go near an airport, and you get to sleep in the same bed every night, so I thought it would suit us both."

"Oh, Ben, are you sure?" Sally asked him.

"Yes," Ben replied. "I think it's time we pushed the boat out." He laughed a little at his own joke. "It was you saying that that made me think of it," he continued. "You've never had a foreign holiday because of old stick-in-the-mud here, so I thought it was time I made an effort."

"But what about the food – it'll all be foreign." Sally picked up the brochure. "Look, Lebanese, Spanish, Italian, Greek. Oh, Ben, it sounds wonderful, but are you really sure?" She looked at him anxiously and he smiled reassuringly.

"It will be wonderful," he told her. "And I think I'm finally getting a bit of a taste for foreign food."

"And I've finally got back my taste for good old-fashioned meals from our childhood," Sally said happily.

"Then," Ben said, taking her into his arms, "we've got the perfect recipe for happiness." Then he held his wife in a long embrace until the smell of burning custard forced him to release her. ■

Finding Prince Charming

J UST look at the muscles in that chest, girls." Sue giggled, quickly rolling bright pink curlers into the front of her red hair. "Where else would you find a pair of shoulders like that? He should be in the films."

Megan nodded shyly, her eyes still glued to the path. Why couldn't Sue just let the subject drop?

"Look at him, June. Isn't he wonderful?" Sue insisted on saying to the third member of their team. "Why, I haven't seen a chest like that since I left our farm."

June giggled agreement behind her hand, then, sensing her friend's rapt attention, she said quietly, "How about you, Megan?"

"Shh, he'll hear you," Megan whispered urgently. "Do you want him to know we've been talking about him behind his back?" She tossed back her blonde hair, her blue eyes flashing in a rare moment of annoyance.

"Don't be silly, Megan," June said, trying to keep a straight face. "Albert wouldn't mind a bit. After all, he already knows he's the finest piece of horse flesh this side of the border, especially with all the coddling he gets from you. You must go through a gallon of apples a week." She put a comforting arm around Megan's shoulders. "Or is it the fine, handsome fellow leading him that's making you blush?"

Megan's colour deepened to a rosy pink and she disappeared under the collar of the green jersey she wore under the regulation dungarees.

June was right, she did find Hector Hammond, leader of their small group of lumberjacks and lumberjills, all too attractive. Although he'd not by word or deed shown any interest in her – or any of the other girls – sometimes there was the occasional smile in his eyes when he glanced at her, but she put that down to sheer imagination.

It wasn't that he was unsociable exactly; he always passed the time of day and ventured a smile as he issued the daily orders, but the rest was business as usual, rapid questions and answers about the felling, trimming and measuring that took up the rest of the day. After that, he and old Albert had their own work to do.

Well, if that meant that Megan's heart beat a solo tattoo, then so be it. How could anyone help what their feelings tumbled them into? Hers had been somersaulted headlong at Hector Hammond as soon as he had first trod that same woodland path.

Every single morning she watched for his dark hair with its faint grey

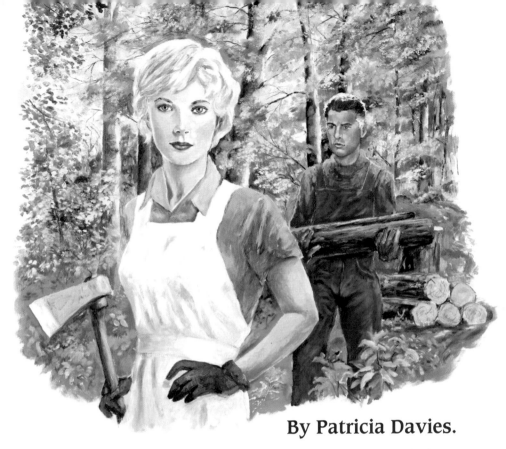

By Patricia Davies.

wings as he carefully led Albert down to the elongated lorries waiting in the open glade at the bottom of the forest. Some timber would go by road, the rest by the river that ran parallel into the estuary, depending on where they were going.

MEGAN sighed as she took out the large measuring tape from her satchel and quickly straddled a fallen tree to measure its girth. At least, she told herself with perverse satisfaction, she had no rivals for his non-existent affections – or none that she knew of, anyway. Only old Albert, of course, the gentle giant he collected each morning from his stable at the base camp. His affection there was very obvious; they doted on each other. How could she be jealous of a horse? She spoiled him rotten herself.

The steady deep thud of axes on wood and the whine of circular saws echoed through the forest for the rest of the day. Hector didn't hold with slacking. His grey-blue eyes could snap quickly enough at anyone found lagging behind with his quota.

If only those same eyes would notice her.

She straightened quickly. Was the diameter of that tree trunk two feet or three? Just see where dreaming of grey eyes got you!

* * * *

"Bags I get first bath tonight," Sue called cheerfully, carefully twisting more pieces of hair around the curlers peeping out from the front of her turban. It was a good job that Hector chose to ignore little feminine touches like this, when it just so happened that there was a jig on at the Odeon tonight and there was a lorry full of giggling girls going from their base.

"You can't have first bath. It's my turn," June called sharply back.

"No, it's not. It's mine," Megan said, "and I really don't mind who has it first, because I don't think I'll bother going anyway."

"Oh, come on, Megan. Just because Hector doesn't usually go himself, there's no point cutting off your nose," June told her. "After all, Prince Charming might show up instead, you never know. There's old Mr Hughes the butcher, who is always sniffing, and, at the very least, there's that short man who keeps bees and whose fingers are always sticky. What more could you want?"

They all laughed, but June put her arm through Megan's in sympathy. Everyone knew what she wanted. Everyone, that is, except Hector Hammond.

Megan was young, very pretty and a really nice girl, who unfortunately wore her heart on her sleeve. Several of the lumberjacks they worked with eyed her with more than a passing interest, but Megan didn't even see them. Still, you never knew, June thought, perhaps she'd be proved right.

B Y the time Megan had urged her tired legs into the Nissen hut they'd been allocated, Sue was already splashing happily behind the screen, wallowing in the small tin bath and revelling in the first turn of really hot water. The only thing she left on was her turban.

June had stretched out on her bed in the corner with her eyes closed, her satisfied sighs coming up from her weary feet, and her cap with the WTC (Women's Timber Corp) badge perched on the bedside table. They were all proud of the work they did. There was a great shortage of timber, as it wasn't easy in this climate for the ships to bring wood from overseas. Still, they all enjoyed the work and the feeling that they were doing something valuable for the war effort.

Some of the lumberjills in their particular part of the forest felled trees alongside the lumberjacks; others prepared the timber, measuring and trimming the trunks. They even had to work on Saturdays, so the odd dance on Saturday night was extra welcome. Especially if Hector Hammond let them finish early and turned a blind eye to numerous curlers hanging out of coloured turbans.

He and Albert often worked late on their own, to cover the work left behind, but tonight even Hector had finished early, so perhaps there was a chance that he'd show up at the dance, even if he didn't stay very long.

Megan sighed and looked at the dress hanging over the cupboard door. She'd loved it as soon as she'd seen it in the shop window. It was quite the prettiest dress she'd ever had, and it had cost her nearly three weeks' pay. She'd bought it especially for the next dance, the one tonight, the excitement rising with each passing day, as she'd envisaged Hector catching sight of her across the dance floor and finally realising his love. Not that he came very often, so it was hardly likely.

Megan sighed heavily. Just how naïve was she? Life seldom ended like in the films. No matter how pretty she made herself look, he obviously preferred old Albert.

Megan ran her hands over the filmy material and smoothed the pale, printed flowers as though they were real blooms. How lovely it was, how feminine, and how she longed to wear it, even if he wasn't even there. After all, she told herself with unusual vigour, she didn't have to wait for Hector Hammond to notice her. Perhaps June was right; perhaps it was time she woke up. Cinderella would go to the ball. Well, the Odeon, anyway.

It was halfway through the second rumba and a night of success for Megan, who had never been without a partner, when disaster struck.

There was a sudden commotion at the entrance door and a couple of late lumberjack boys dashed into the hall, their trousers wet up to their knees.

"We need help at the river," one shouted above the sound of the music. "Old Albert's managed to fall down the bank and it's too slippery for him to climb out. Even with Hector Hammond there, he's panicking and he won't let anyone near him. The river will soon be over the bank."

"We're going back with the lorry, but I doubt he'll let us put a harness on him," the other said. "We've already tried, and he's a mite heavy to haul out, anyway. We're going back to see what else we can do. Who wants a lift?"

THE hall emptied in moments, men and girls from the base quickly filling the large vehicle, dancing forgotten.

Megan's heart raced as she crouched in the back of the lorry. What was Hector doing? He'd be devastated if anything happened to Albert.

June quickly squeezed her friend's hand, and even in the darkness she could feel Megan's tension.

"Try not to worry, love, Hector will sort it out – he always does, doesn't he? Tomorrow we'll be feeding our Albert an apple and chiding him for getting himself into this pickle."

Megan could only nod dumbly.

The moon lay hidden behind the clouds, so only the splashing beyond the bank led them to where the big horse lay half submerged in the water. This wasn't the quiet, docile animal they were used to; this was a plunging, panic-stricken black shadow that threw up water and mud as he rolled and dug with his hooves at the slippery bank that refused to let him go. Every move upward brought him slithering back again.

He was tiring rapidly as the remorseless river, so near to the sea, continued to rise, the ripples racing past almost to their full height.

Megan saw Hector at once, crouched in the river alongside the horse, a black shadow that never moved from Albert, his arms around the animal's neck and his soft voice crooning encouragement at each effort that brought Albert sliding back again.

Others came closer to try to help, but Albert only struggled more and wouldn't let them near, his eyes rolling and white with fear. If only he could get a firm grip on the bank for a few paces, he'd be over it and safe. If only . . .

Megan didn't know where the idea came from, or if it would only make matters worse. Only Hector would know if it could work.

Heedless of the cold and the water, she walked a few paces away from the horse, took off her silver dancing shoes, then slid down the bank and carefully moved through the freezing water towards Hector and Albert.

HECTOR'S tired face was white with cold and fear. Albert snorted and threw his great head around, but he knew the one who fed him so many apples and his head fell back again into the mud. Megan crouched down beside Hector Hammond and slowly smoothed the huge animal's neck.

Man and horse were both too tired to do anything but lie there gasping for breath.

How would Albert get the energy to do any more? But he was going to have to, for her plan to succeed.

"Hector." The pale face turned towards her. "Albert can't get up the bank because it's too slippery for him to get a grip, isn't that so? Her beautiful dance dress floated upwards in the muddy water, but Megan didn't even notice.

"What if the bank wasn't muddy, Hector?" He looked at her without comprehension. "The rushes just over the top are dry, and there are plenty of them. If we can get enough of them to cover the slope and sink into the mud, they would make a firmer surface for Albert to grip on to.

"We could cover them with grass, branches, pieces of left-over timber, anything. It's worth a try, isn't it? What do you think?"

Hector didn't answer, but suddenly his tired eyes flew open and he was barking orders upwards into the crowd standing silently above them.

Suddenly the crowd scattered in the dark, tearing up rushes, collecting branches – anything that would make a firmer barrier for Albert to climb, while Megan and Hector waited in the river. Hector gently touched the cold

Slapton Sands

SLAPTON SANDS in South Devon is unusual in that it is a very popular and picturesque beach, but it also plays an important part in the survival of some of the UK's rarest flora and fauna. The Nature Reserve is packed with wildlife and the freshwater lake, Slapton Ley, means that the plants and animals vary according to the season. This, of course, guarantees that you will see something different every time you visit.

It was on this beach in 1943 that the Allied Forces staged a rehearsal for the D-Day landings. Unfortunately, a combination of live ammunition and poor visibility resulted in the deaths of 749 American servicemen. There is a stone monument set in place on Slapton Sands to commemorate the ill-fated "Operation Tiger", and a Sherman tank at nearby Torcross.

Corner Shop

THE curly bell on the sweetshop door
Signified a treat in store.
With a penny in your hand,
A passport to a wonderland,
Sherbert dabs and toffee bars,
Shelves and shelves of sweets in jars;
And all the captivating smells
Cast their weekly magic spells,
Where spirits soared to dizzy heights
In that world of sweet delights.
Tho' that was oh, so long ago,
The memories still ebb and flow.
I close my eyes and still can see
That corner shop of sweets and me . . .

– Brian H. Gent.

hand that lay beside his on the horse's neck.

"I . . . I'm not one for many words, Megan." As if she didn't know. "But I've admired you for a long time."

Was she really hearing this, standing in a muddy river?

"It's been agony seeing you every day. I didn't know how to tell you that . . . that I've been married before, but it just didn't work out. She preferred someone else. Anyway, I think that I'm just too old for you, Megan, that's why I just couldn't ask you before . . . I mean, if you'd like to . . . ?"

"Of course I will, Hector, I'd really love to."

"You would?"

She nodded happily, frozen to the marrow.

THE bank, when at last they looked up, was filling with timber and rushes pressed firmly into the mud. By now the river was flooding dramatically. Hector gave Albert the signal to move and, revived after his rest, Albert put his front hooves on the firmer slope, and, after one slide backwards when everyone held their breath, he bounded upwards and over the top to the cheers of the large crowd that had gathered to watch.

Hector and Megan stood together, hand in hand, oblivious to their surroundings.

"Well," Sue whispered, satisfaction dripping from every word. "What do you think happened there, then?"

"Well, we'll probably never know." June laughed. "But if you're thinking of getting your man to propose, just find a freezing, muddy river, a very large horse and plenty of people to watch. Now, let's go back to the dance, shall we?" ■

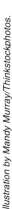

No Place Like Home

by Samantha Tonge.

ACE glowing from the breezy bicycle ride down the village high street, Tilly applied the brakes and turned left into Acacia Avenue. She came to a halt outside the third cottage on the right. Postcard perfect, it belonged to her grandparents. She dismounted and pushed her bicycle up to the front door. She rang the bell and after waiting a few minutes, laid her bicycle on the ground and made her way around to the back.

"Yoo, hoo, dear, over here," Pauline called from the bottom of the garden.

Tilly crossed the lawn and gave her gran a hug.

"It's a fab day for a bike ride," Tilly said, and gazed down at her pasty legs, sticking out of her denim shorts. "Perhaps I'll get a tan, even though we're not going abroad."

It was the beginning of the Whitsun holiday week off school and, obligingly, rays of sun had broken through the cloud.

"You're just in time for a cup of tea and a scone," Pauline said. "Grandpa is inside, trying to mend the tumble dryer. I've promised to launder the dirty

Healing Green

PALE green and dark green, moss
green and lime,
So many summer shades,
In cottage gardens, hills and dales
And all the leafy glades.
The gentle green of summer days
In sunlight or in rain,
Can touch the heart and calm the mind
In street or country lane.

The city dwellers cherish plants
In window-box or pot,
And now and then escape to toil
In some suburban plot.
Dame Nature gives year-round
delight
With every changing scene,
But nothing soothes the human soul
So much as healing green.

– Iris Hesselden.

tablecloths and tea towels from the church fête next Saturday, so I hope the good weather doesn't turn before then. Mother Nature is the best dryer around. Talking of which, how about you help me hang out my washing?"

TILLY followed her gran inside, through the kitchen back door. Twenty minutes later, skirts and shirts hung on the line, while she and her grandparents basked in the sun. A greenfinch hopped across the patio and under the garden furniture to peck at crumbs of scone.

"What have you got planned for this week?" her grandpa asked, after he'd wiped his mouth with a napkin.

Tilly shrugged.

"Nothing much. With exams coming up next year I've got plenty of homework, but I'm just going to chill for a few days first."

"Are you meeting up with Becca?" Pauline asked. "I take it you two are still best friends and haven't had another fall-out?"

Tilly grinned back.

"Yes, we're still talking, even though I'm mad she's been allowed to dye her hair first."

"Fourteen is far too young for all those unnatural chemicals, and your hair is such a pretty colour anyway," Gran pronounced.

Bob almost choked on his mouthful of tea.

"If I remember correctly, Pauline, my love, you were Tilly's age when your fair curls suddenly turned a dark shade of brown."

"Gran!" Tilly exclaimed.

Pauline's cheeks tinged pink.

"My parents were furious. I'd saved my pocket money for weeks and my friend Jean and I each bought a home-colouring kit from the chemist. We wanted to look like Audrey Hepburn in 'Breakfast At Tiffany's'."

"You could compete with any Hollywood star, Pauline, just the way you were," Bob said softly.

"Yes, remember when we looked through those old albums, Gran?" Tilly asked. "Your beehive hairstyle looked amazing and I really loved those winkle-picker shoes."

"So, are you going shopping with Becca, then, love?" Bob asked Tilly, with a wink at his wife, who always felt uncomfortable with compliments. "Tell me the day and I'll give you a lift to save on bus fares."

The teenager's shoulders sagged.

"No. She's in Italy with her family. Imagine that – visiting the fashion centre of Europe. And Megan has gone to France . . ."

Her grandparents exchanged looks.

"Well, never mind, dear," Pauline said briskly. "Why don't you come here tomorrow? I'll plan something special."

"Oh, don't worry about me," Tilly mumbled. "I'm just being daft."

"We know things have been hard since your mum's hours were cut," Pauline said as she poured out a second cup of tea for everyone.

Tilly sighed.

"Yep. Plus Dad's always worrying about the price of petrol, what with his delivery job. But I shouldn't complain, some of my friends are a lot worse off. Callum and his family had to move into a smaller house last month.

"I don't expect exotic holidays." She stretched out her arm. "Still, a bit of fake tan might do the job . . ."

"I read somewhere that white is the new brown," Pauline commented.

Tilly groaned.

"That's exactly what Mum said."

NEXT morning, Tilly rose bright and early to another cloudless sky. After helping her mum bake and freeze a batch of scones, she cycled through the village once more to her grandparents' home. The cheery ride was just the tonic she needed to lift her spirits after the text she'd received from Becca, extolling Italy's amazing cafés and shops.

"Afternoon, Gran." Tilly kissed Pauline on the cheek as she walked in.

She slipped off her pumps and listened for a moment. What sort of music was that?

Pauline was grinning as she took Tilly's hand and led her into the lounge.

What on earth was her grandpa doing? Arms outstretched, he kicked with alternate feet to the beat which gradually sped up.

"I didn't know you had it in you," Tilly said. "Have you been out in the sun too long?" She gave an impish grin.

"Less of your cheek, missy," he said, slightly out of breath. "We are learning how to dance Greek style. Travelling abroad might not be an option at the moment, but that doesn't mean your week can't take an exotic turn. Come on, Tilly, join in the fun."

Pauline clapped her hands to the music.

"First off, we'll learn Zorba's dance, then the three of us will prepare a themed Greek dinner."

"Salad with olives and feta cheese to start," Bob announced enthusiastically. "Followed by moussaka."

Pauline smiled as Bob slipped his arm around her shoulders.

"I drove into town this morning," he continued. "The big supermarket sells Greek pastries called *Baklava*. We'll have these for pudding."

Tilly giggled as the two grandparents jigged up and down.

"You could have at least drawn the curtains."

"Come on, dear." Pauline waved her over and with a chuckle, put her arm around Tilly's shoulders. "Teenagers should be able to let their hair down."

A FTER a considerable amount of persuasion, Tilly followed the moves, building up speed with the music, just like her grandpa. Bob had found a website on his PC which demonstrated exactly what to do, and within half an hour, Tilly really began to enjoy herself. In fact, Pauline and Bob had to beg her to stop when, exhausted, knees and backs aching, they declared it was time to head into the garden for a break.

"Hmm, this home-made lemonade is the best." Tilly sipped appreciatively and put on her sunglasses. "I can't wait to start cooking. That moussaka sounds yummy."

"Agreed," Bob concurred and mopped his perspiring brow. "I can't remember the last time I ate aubergine."

"Oh, it was probably when we visited Spain for our ruby wedding anniversary," Pauline told him. "Remember that lovely little restaurant near the beach? Its speciality was aubergine and sausage casserole. We ate that a couple of times, and had a jug of sangria, too."

"Did you go abroad much at my age?" Tilly asked.

"Oh, no." Pauline shook her head. "Not many people did in those days. Flights cost too much. My auntie lived in Skegness and we visited her for two weeks every summer. I have many fond memories of collecting cockles. I'd help Auntie scrub them clean and, after boiling them, we'd sprinkle on parsley and serve them with lemon."

Tilly pulled a face.

"Mum and Dad would treat us to candy floss and we'd eat fish and chips out of the newspaper," Pauline continued. "Every year Mum made me a new sundress for the beach, and when I was younger there'd be a hat to match. She was a whiz with a needle and thread."

She put down her glass.

"You stayed in a hotel, didn't you, Bob?"

He nodded.

"It was more of a bed and breakfast really – on the sea front in Bournemouth. We had the same room every year. Mum loved it; said it was a real holiday for her, because she didn't have to rush around in the morning, boiling eggs and making toast soldiers.

"One year we even managed to afford a holiday camp. Mum didn't have to cook a single meal. The entertainment was brilliant." Bob shook his head and grinned. "Dad won the knock-knees competition."

"Talking about cooking," Pauline interrupted, "we need to get on with dinner. Bob, could you pick some tomatoes for the salad? Come on, Tilly, let's chop the veg."

THE rest of the afternoon flew past and at six sharp the doorbell rang and in walked Tilly's mum and dad, who had also been invited for tea. The food was delicious and, when they'd all eaten, they made Greek iced coffees and carried them into the lounge.

"Now for the perfect way to finish off our day!" Pauline nodded to Bob, who pressed play on the DVD machine. It was "Mamma Mia".

"I love this movie," Tilly declared. "Every time I watch it, I promise myself that one day I'll move to a Greek island."

By the time the credits rolled, everyone else agreed with her.

Bob and Pauline rose, stretched their stiff joints and, to hoots of laughter, danced to the last Abba songs. Tilly caught sight of a faded cross-stitch picture on the wall. Her gran had sewn it years ago, when she and Bob bought the cottage. It read, *There's No Place Like Home*.

"Thanks for a cool time," Tilly said to her grandparents after another round of iced coffee and *Baklava*. It had been great to see Dad so relaxed and Mum giggling at Grandpa's moves.

Pauline smiled.

"These surroundings can't match fashionable Italy, Tilly, but I hope today's been a change from the usual routine."

Tilly nodded and leaned her head against her mum's shoulder. Once again she gazed at the faded cross-stitch picture. Yes, she would still love to join Becca, strolling past boutiques in Rome, but staying at home for the holidays was under-rated. In fact, she couldn't wait for tomorrow. Gran and Grandpa had invited her around again. They'd muttered something about paella and digging out their old souvenir Spanish castanets . . . ■

Independence Day

by Christine Barnes.

SEVENTEEN years old. A-levels just completed. Summer holiday to Greece with friends booked.

Jen's stomach twisted as she gazed at her daughter, Becky, who was reading on the sofa. It didn't seem possible that her bonnie baby was now ready to fly the nest. In September she'd be off to university. She'd be one of the youngest in the year.

Perhaps that was why Jen found it difficult to let go, having always protected her August baby from the rough and tumble of older children. Except that she wasn't a small child any more.

Becky grinned and put down her book.

"Mum, have I got chocolate around my mouth?"

Jen picked up her sewing and raised her eyebrows.

"You've been staring at me for the last five minutes," Becky said.

Jen's cheeks tinged pink.

"Sorry, love. It's just nice to have you home all day now that your exams have finished. I bet you're looking forward to your trip with Jess and Kristin."

"I can't wait! My first-ever holiday abroad on my own. Not that I haven't enjoyed my holidays with you and Dad, but . . ."

"I understand, love," Jen said, a twinkle in her eye. Clearly, she recalled her own first teenage trip abroad in the Eighties, to Spain, especially the prettily garnished cocktails and legs burned red from the Mediterranean sun.

"You will be careful, won't you?" Jen said, the lines around her eyes deeper than usual. "Keep your purse and phone hidden and turn down lifts from strangers. Be sure to wear a helmet if you hire one of those mopeds."

Illustration by Mandy Dixon/Thinkstockphotos.

Becky groaned.

"Mum, please. I'm an adult now. Or I will be by then. In fact, I must start planning my birthday bash."

Jen nodded. Becky would leave for Greece during the first week of August, two days after she turned eighteen. And she had to admit, regardless of age, Becky was a responsible girl who never forgot her money for taxis and always rang home if she was running late.

But she still liked a hug first thing every morning and bought sweets as a treat – the chewy ones, in the shape of fried eggs. They'd been her favourite for years.

"Talking of parties . . ." Becky continued. "You know Kristin's mum?"

"Yes, I meant to ask how Cindy was doing this week, love. Did she try walking without her stick, at last?"

Becky nodded and tucked a glossy strand of brown hair behind her ear.

"She almost managed it. The doctors are very pleased with her progress, apparently, after such a bad car crash. She asked me to thank you again for all the home cooking you've been sending over."

"It was the least I could do." Jen had been glad to be of assistance. With a broken leg to manoeuvre, Cindy hadn't been able to cook much from scratch.

"She said it made a real difference. In fact, I've found my own way to help out, too."

Becky stood up and paced the room.

"What with Kristin's family being American, you know how they always have a big party for Independence Day?"

"Yes. Last year's was a hoot, asking us all to dress up as famous Americans." Jen chuckled. "Your dad took a real liking to that cowboy hat."

"Well, Independence Day is two weeks on Saturday and Cindy's really disappointed that she won't be up to organising any celebrations. So, I suggested to Kristin that she and I plan a party as a surprise. Her dad thinks it's a great idea. What do you reckon?"

"That's very thoughtful, Becky!

71

I could help with catering, if you like. Why don't we make a list?"

"It's OK, thanks, Mum," Becky said. "I've got plenty of time on my hands, now, and when she's not doing the cooking and housework for her mum, Kristin will help. We've got this idea for a large cake, in the shape of a flag, using blueberries and raspberries to mark out the American stars and stripes."

"Oh, that sounds impressive," Jen said.

"Jess said she'll bake some of her fab chocolate brownies," Becky continued. "I'm going to research fancy salads on the internet. Kristin will make her mum's famous American coleslaw and cornbread. Kristin's dad will do a barbecue on the day and he'll cover all costs. I just hope we can keep it a secret from Cindy, at least until the morning of the fourth."

"You seem to have thought of everything, love," Jen said brightly. "But if you need my help, you know where I am."

"Thanks, Mum." Becky got up and kissed her on the cheek. "I'm sure we'll be fine. In fact, I'd better go and log on to the internet now. Two weeks isn't that long."

Nor is 18 years, Jen thought, a slight lump in her throat as she carried on with her sewing.

Confident Becky seemed to have everything under control. Which was good, Jen told herself. Her daughter would need to be organised for life on her own at university.

TRUE to form, two weeks later, the girls' hard work had paid off. Despite all the preparations, Cindy still didn't suspect a thing. It was the day before the party and Becky and Kristin had just got back from the strawberry fields to wash the fruit at Jen's house. Yet the look on her daughter's face gave Jen cause for concern.

"Look outside, Mum," Becky said. "I've never seen such dark clouds."

"But all week the forecasters have said we're in for an awesome weekend," Kristin said in her Texan drawl. "It was a sure thing, or so they said."

Becky shrugged.

"Didn't you listen to the news on the car radio? After this week's hot weather they are now predicting storms and torrential rain."

"Yes, I heard that this morning," Jen said. "I was hoping they'd got it wrong."

"What will we do?" Kristin bit her lip. "At this late notice, we can't have everyone indoors. Mom would fret that the place wasn't clean enough, and it's a mammoth job to move all the furniture."

Becky looked at her watch.

"We've got all this fruit to wash and the cake still to bake. We'll never find a marquee tent for hire with only twenty-four hours to go."

"Deep breaths," Jen said with a calm smile, taken back for a few seconds

72

Fifty Years Ago . . . **July 27, 1964**

THIS day, 50 years ago, saw Winston Churchill make his final appearance in the House of Commons. He was just a few months short of his ninetieth birthday when his political career, which had begun in 1900 when he was successfully returned as MP for Oldham, drew to a close. His career included being Prime Minister twice, memorably leading Britain through the dark days of WWII, when his speeches and radio broadcasts helped inspire the British people.

Churchill was also an officer in the British Army, an historian, a writer and an artist. He is the only British prime minister to have received the Nobel Prize in Literature, and was made an Honorary Citizen of the United States by President John F. Kennedy. He was the first person to be given this honour.

On his death in January 1965, Churchill was granted the honour of a state funeral in St Paul's Cathedral and lay in state for three days. He is buried in the family plot near Blenheim Palace, where he was born.

73

to Becky, aged ten. She'd just received the date for her first-ever piano exam and was convinced she didn't have enough time to practise. "I'll make you two sandwiches first. You can't troubleshoot on an empty stomach. After lunch, girls, bake your cake, whilst I wash the fruit."

"But what about tomorrow? What about the weather?" Becky said. "It's too late to cancel. And we can't let all that food go to waste. Kristin's neighbours have hidden all the barbecue meat in their freezers and loads of salad ingredients are in the garage." Becky gazed at all the strawberries and shook her head.

"Don't you worry," Jen said. "It'll be all right. I've got an idea . . ."

SATURDAY, July 4 dawned bright and sunny, yet sure enough, by the time guests arrived at midday, fat raindrops tumbled out of the sky. "What would I do without you, Mum? And thank goodness for the church," Becky said with a wink, before circulating amongst the guests with a tray of drinks.

Jen smiled. Yes, her experience of helping out at church events had come in useful, after all. Reverend Higgins was always prepared for every scenario, and over the years had accumulated a rather grand collection of gazebos. Becky and Kristin's dads had erected the largest for the guests, and a smaller one to cover the barbecue. Fortunately, it was a warm day, with no wind to blow rain sideways, so everyone could still wear their summery outfits. Jen thought how grown-up Becky looked in her halter-neck top and smart sandals.

"Aren't our gals amazing, Jen?" Cindy drawled as she managed to hobble over holding her glass, a red, white and blue ribbon tied around the walking stick hanging from her arm. "I almost keeled over when the girls sprung this on me after breakfast. Quite the nicest surprise I've had in my life. I love that stars and stripes cake." She smiled. "Becky's a credit to you, honey. Between you and me, I was worried about the Greek trip until I knew your daughter was going along. She's got a real sensible head on her."

Jen's cheeks glowed.

"Thanks, Cindy. I am proud, as you should be, too. Kristin's a lovely girl."

Cindy nodded.

"Reckon us parents have done a good job, raising our kids to be independent. Isn't that what it's all about?"

Cindy's words ringing in her ears, Jen gazed across the lawn at Becky. Her American friend was right, and really, Jen had known this for a while, watching Becky revise for her exams lately and seeing how she sailed through her university interview.

Jen clinked glasses with Cindy and waved to Becky, who was still busy handing out summer punch. Independence Day really was something to celebrate this year. ■

Illustration by Gerard Fay.

by Pat Posner.

Mistaken Identity

YOUR babies will be fine for ten minutes, Teagan." Stephanie smiled as the golden retriever cast anxious looks back at the large puppy pen situated in the shade of a weeping willow tree. "Come on, girl, we'll just walk around the green."

Busy encouraging Teagan to follow her, Stephanie didn't notice the car parked outside number nine until she opened her garden gate. Maybe the new people are moving in at last, she thought. It had only just turned eight o'clock, so either it was someone fairly local or else they'd set off at the crack of dawn.

The *SOLD* notice had been in place for over four months but, amazingly, none of the Cresslethwaite villagers knew who'd bought Honeypot Cottage. Stephanie sneaked a few furtive glances as she walked past, but couldn't see anyone.

Mentally shrugging, she meandered along Ernswick Fold – a sort of horseshoe shape with the green in the centre. She really enjoyed this early morning walk with Teagan and today everything seemed particularly beautiful. The distant corn fields were splashed with the vivid scarlet of corn poppies, the air was already full of scent from buttercups, daisies, clover, meadowsweet and lady's slipper, and the lime trees around the green seemed to be waiting patiently for the bees to visit.

"Hi, Steph. Isn't it gorgeous weather?" Polly Lumb, who lived diagonally opposite Stephanie, came through her garden gate carrying a covered basket.

"Must be the best July we've had for years," Stephanie replied.

"So what are the newcomers like?" Polly pointed across the green. "That car must belong to them. There's no way the estate agent would be here this early."

Stephanie shrugged.

"I couldn't see anyone when I walked past. Where are you off to, Polly?"

"I'm taking some goats' cheese to Sally so she can make some of her special tartlets for Little Teapot's Cream-tea Tuesday. Here, Steph, hold my basket a minute while I stroke Teagan."

"I think she's anxious to get back to her puppies," Stephanie said. "I'm going to cut our walk short and go back over the green."

"And that way you'll make sure you won't miss seeing who comes out of Honeypot Cottage!" Polly's eyes sparkled with laughter and Stephanie smiled.

"You know me too well. Of course, this hot weather means that I will have to water my front garden later. If there's anyone around, I'll definitely see them then."

"Good, you can tell me all about them over a cream tea this afternoon. You are coming, aren't you?"

"I am. And I'll bring your sweater, Poll. I finished the latest lot yesterday. I washed them in baby shampoo and they dried overnight. They're on their racks in the back garden now, airing off."

"Still getting plenty of orders?"

Steph nodded and crossed her fingers. It had been scary setting up her designer sweater business, but so far, things were looking good.

"I've been really lucky. I just hope I don't get too many orders for my huge butterfly motif, though. The sweater I finished yesterday nearly gave me a nervous breakdown. Yours with the goats was much easier."

Polly smiled.

"It's great running a business from home if it works out well."

THERE still wasn't any sign of her new neighbours when Stephanie reached her front gate, but then she heard what sounded like a young boy's voice. Teagan pricked up her ears before moving quickly towards the back garden. Stephanie followed and opened the puppy pen door to let her in.

"I'm going to make a drink, then I'll package up a few sweaters and go to post them," she said as she watched Teagan settle happily with her pups.

An hour later when Stephanie walked into the post office and general store, Marion Fawcett was serving a tall, dark-haired man and a young boy.

"Ah," Marion said with a smile, "here is Miss Evans, your next-door neighbour. Stephanie, this is Mr Hunt and his son, Matthew."

Hoping her smile would be seen as a greeting, when really it was amusement because Marion appeared to be using her "posh" voice, Stephanie greeted the newcomers.

"Andrew," the man said. "It's nice to meet you, Miss Evans."

"She makes and sells designer knitwear," Marion told him. "And her golden retriever just had puppies a few weeks ago. She'll probably let you see my little Angel when you move in, Matthew."

"We just came to measure up for curtains today," Andrew Hunt explained. "We'll be moving in on Friday. Excuse me if we hurry off now – I've got to get to work."

"I hope the move goes well," Stephanie said. "Come round if you need anything, or if Matthew wants to see the puppies."

As Andrew opened the shop door, Matthew darted back and tugged Stephanie's arm.

"It's seven in your garden, isn't it?" he whispered.

"Yes, it is." Stephanie nodded.

"Wow," he said. Then, mumbling something Stephanie didn't catch, he hurried out after his dad.

"Matthew must have looked out of the window and counted Teagan's puppies. He was just telling me that there were seven puppies in my garden." Stephanie smiled as she passed her parcels over the counter to Marion.

"Maybe the Hunts will buy one of them, Stephanie. Be nice for you to have one of Teagan's puppies living next door as well as here." Marion sounded more like her usual self now. "I can hardly wait to come and collect Angel."

Stephanie laughed.

"She's the most mischievous of the lot. You might not think her quite so angelic when you get her home."

Andrew Hunt drove past as she walked homewards. He gave her a wave, as did the red-haired woman in the passenger seat. His wife looks nice, Stephanie thought, returning the wave and feeling pleased that she'd have a little bit of news for Polly and the other villagers.

FRIDAY dawned warmer than ever. Worried in case the afternoon sun was too hot for the puppies, Stephanie put them in their indoor pen.

"I'll let you out to run around the kitchen after I've tidied the garden," she told them, laughing as they jumped around.

"Are you coming with me, Teagan?" she asked.

But Teagan, after barking back at her pups, flopped down outside the pen.

"OK, stay and keep an eye on them. I'll be back in soon."

Stephanie was about to move the outdoor pen when, through the willow tree's drooping branches, she saw Matthew at the far end of the garden.

"I'm looking for Mummy," Matthew said as Stephanie approached him with a cheerful greeting.

"Isn't she in your house, Matthew?"

"Course not. She's here somewhere. In heaven."

"She's where?"

"Mummy's here in heaven. You said heaven's in your garden. I thought it was, because I saw my mummy's jumper – the one with the huge butterfly on. And you're Miss Heaven and you've got angels, that other lady in the shop said so."

"I . . ." Stephanie didn't know what to say.

She thought back to the day in the shop and recalled Matthew's whispered words – "It's seven in your garden". She'd thought he was talking about the puppies. But he must have said heaven, not seven. And Marion had mentioned the puppy she was having. The puppy she'd already named Angel. And if Matthew's mum was in heaven that meant . . .

Matthew interrupted her chaotic thoughts.

"Do you think I will see her, Miss Heaven? Have you seen her?"

"Oh, sweetheart, I think you . . ." Stephanie stopped mid-flow. How could she explain to this sweet little boy that he'd got everything so wrong? She guessed he was only five or six. Should she take him home? Surely his dad would have noticed his son was missing by now?

"I've brought this." Matthew reached into a pocket and handed Stephanie a crumpled photo of a toddler in a buggy and an attractive dark-haired woman wearing a sweater with a butterfly motif on it. It was very similar to the one Stephanie had put out to air in the garden on Tuesday.

"So is this you in the buggy?" Stephanie asked.

Matthew nodded, took the photo back and pointed.

"And that's my mummy. I brought the photo so she'll know who I am," he said. "She's been in heaven a very long time and I've grown lots bigger."

Before Stephanie had the chance to say anything, someone shouted Matthew's name.

"I'm here, Daddy – in heaven's garden," Matthew called back.

IT couldn't have been more than a couple of minutes before Andrew Hunt arrived, but it seemed like a lifetime to Stephanie. He looked down at his son, frowning.

"Matthew, I told you to stay in our garden," he scolded him, before glancing at Stephanie and apologising.

"I came looking for Mummy," Matthew mumbled.

Andrew hunkered down in front of his son.

"But, Matt," he said huskily, "we've spoken about this. You know your mum's . . ."

"In heaven. And it's heaven in this garden." He pointed at Stephanie. "Miss Heaven said it was. And my mummy's butterfly jumper was here. She must have got too hot and took it off."

"Miss Evans," Andrew rose in one fluid movement, "I'm not really sure what's happened here, but I can only apologise again for Matthew disturbing you."

He put an arm around Matthew's shoulders.

"Auntie Linda has finished putting up your bookcase, so you can put all your books and stuff on the shelves."

Stephanie felt that she owed Matthew's father some sort of explanation.

"Mr Hunt, I think I might have a clue how this mix-up happened."

"You do? And do you have an idea of how to put it right, Miss Evans?"

She shook her head.

"The mind can play funny tricks when you've lost someone. It takes a long time to accept that you'll never see them again. I think I understand how Matthew . . ." She shook her head. "No, I don't. He's just a child. My experience is different from his."

Stephanie swallowed hard. All of this was a bit close to home.

"I'm sorry," she muttered.

"Look," he said, his expression softening, "how about I take Matthew round to my sister and then come back here and we'll talk about it?"

Stephanie nodded.

"I'll be in the kitchen. Teagan might bark when you come in, but she's a big softie really."

✳ ✳ ✳ ✳

"So, that's how Matthew came to think my garden's heaven."

Stephanie had explained it as best as she could while she and Andrew sat at the kitchen table with drinks of home-made lemonade.

"It's an unhappy coincidence there were seven puppies in the garden, and Marion Fawcett does tend to add an aitch to my name," she concluded.

Andrew nodded.

"I can see now how Matt must have added it all up. I'm sorry if I seemed a bit brusque."

"That's all right, Mr Hunt. Really it is. I was upset, but you must have felt a hundred times worse than I did."

"I was more worried about Matt, to be honest."

"He was quite matter of fact about it when he told me why he was in my garden. He didn't seem to be distressed in the slightest." Stephanie took a biscuit and pushed the plate across to Matthew's dad.

"It's three years since Jessica died. It was a road accident and Matt was only two. I don't really know if I was right trying to keep her memory alive for him. I certainly didn't expect anything like this to happen."

"Maybe you've been keeping her memory alive for yourself, as well," Stephanie said. "Sometimes that feels like the only way to cope. My Gary was a fireman. He died a week before our wedding after rescuing a baby from a house fire. That was five years ago and I still find it hard to accept at times."

"Things hit you unexpectedly, don't they? I thought I'd accepted Jessica's death, but maybe you're right. Perhaps keeping her memory alive has been as much for me as for Matt. And for my sister, too. She's living with us while her husband's abroad. Linda and Jessica were best friends, you see."

"You haven't done anything wrong. It can only be a good thing for Matthew to know he had a mum who loved him."

"I'll try to explain it all to him tonight. He can't go on thinking your garden is heaven. I just hope I can get it right."

STEPHANIE reached for the jug of lemonade and poured them both another glass.

"I'm sure you will. And if Matthew wants to keep coming in my garden, I don't mind. As long as he gets permission from you or your sister first."

"You might regret inviting Matt round. You do realise he won't be going to school until September? He might want to visit you every day for the next five weeks."

Stephanie looked over at the puppies in their pen.

"The pups are the right age now for one or two of the villagers' children to come round for half an hour or so a day to play with them. Matthew could come at the same time. Being with the pups and with other children in the garden might be good for him."

"It would certainly give him other things to think and talk about."

Stephanie nodded.

"It's worth a try, isn't it? Perhaps the three of you would like to come round for a meal tomorrow? Settling into a new house is hard work. Not having to make a meal will be one less thing for you or Linda to think about. Besides," she added, "I'd really like to hear how your chat with Matthew goes."

"That would be good. Thank you. And I don't just mean for the invitation. Thank you for listening and talking. It's really helped."

"It's helped me as well. I can't remember the last time I talked about Gary to anyone. People get embarrassed because they don't know what to say."

"Yes, I find that, too," he agreed. "But, listen, do you think you could call me Andrew? Just to show you've forgiven me for thinking you were in some way to blame for Matthew's mistake."

She thought she'd be able to forgive this gentle, kind man anything.

"You'd better call me Stephanie or Steph, then. I am definitely not Miss Heaven."

Andrew smiled.

"Time will tell, Steph, but I've a feeling we might be about to find our own little patch of heaven on earth."

After she'd seen Andrew out, Stephanie leaned over the puppy pen to stroke Teagan.

"You know what, girl? I've a feeling Andrew might just be right." ∎

MARTIN struggled for breath as he forced one foot in front of the other. He was attempting to get around the track at a pace that vaguely resembled running, but he wasn't doing too well. Each step he took required a supreme effort, the pain in his muscles nearly making him pass out.

It wasn't a good idea for an overweight, out-of-shape man to be running this fast. Particularly as he'd never been sporty, not even as a youngster.

"OK." Heather's voice reached him above the pounding of his heart. "That's a bit of an improvement."

He staggered to the edge of the track.

"I think I've overdone it this time." He was gasping as she approached, brandishing the stop watch. "I'm seeing spots before my eyes."

The race he was training for was a short one by normal standards, but it might as well have been a marathon as far as Martin was concerned.

"Nonsense." Heather was having none of it. "You're doing brilliantly. Rest for a moment and then we'll try it again."

A Good Sport

by Suzanne Jones.

Illustration by Kirk Houston/Thinkstockphotos.

As his breathing returned to near normal, he was relieved to feel the pain in his chest begin to subside. Probably a stitch, rather than anything more serious, he decided.

"I'm still not sure this is a good idea," he said.

Heather raised an eyebrow.

"Can you think of a better one?"

He frowned. He couldn't. But it was more complicated than that.

"Won't Robbie think I'm trying to replace his dad?"

Heather sighed.

"I admit I was worried about that, too. But Mike died before Robbie was born. Robbie's never had anyone to cheer on in the dads' race before. And lots of the children have stepfathers taking part."

Martin began to jog on the spot in an attempt to stop his muscles cooling down and stiffening. He knew what Heather said was true, but he was still worried. Where Robbie was concerned, he just couldn't seem to win. The way things were going, Martin's performance was going to be a monumental embarrassment to everyone concerned.

"I just don't want to do the wrong thing again."

"You know how he feels about sports," Heather reminded him. "This might give you some common ground."

IN the year he and Heather had been married, Martin had tried everything he could think of to make friends with Robbie. But the boy had been unimpressed with it all: fishing trips, visits to the cinema and the zoo. He'd even ignored the expensive pair of football boots Martin had bought him for his birthday.

Perhaps if Martin had children of his own – or even if he shared Robbie's interest in sport – he might have known how to relate to the eight-year-old. But as it was, he was clueless.

Heather sighed.

"I just don't know why it's taking him so long to get used to the situation. He was fine when we were dating. I spoke to him about us getting married and he was very happy."

"It's understandable." Martin took her hand and gave it a supportive squeeze. "It was just the two of you for all those years and then I came along and had the cheek to marry his mother."

"I often wonder if I should have moved back to live near my family when Mike died." Heather bit her lip, pondering, remembering that sad time. "But that would have meant looking for a new job on top of everything else . . ."

"Well, I'm glad you didn't move away," Martin told her as he prepared to do another lap of the track.

"Me, too." Heather smiled. "But it might have been easier on Robbie if there had been other family members around."

"Perhaps," Mike agreed.

With a sigh of resignation, he resumed his training. Making Heather and Robbie happy was his priority now. And if there was a chance that running in the dads' race at Robbie's school would help achieve that, he had to give it a go, however uncomfortable the experience might be for him.

T HEY collected Robbie from his friend's house on the way home. "Did you have a nice time?" Martin asked as the boy buckled his seat belt.

"Yes, thank you," Robbie replied with unfailing politeness, his face serious and unsmiling.

It might have been better if Robbie was rude or disobedient, but he wasn't. He was a lovely boy. It was just that he was quiet and reserved – and he hadn't accepted Martin as part of the family.

"Why don't you go for a shower, Martin?" Heather suggested when they arrived home. "I'll have dinner heated through by the time you get down. I've prepared your favourite – cottage pie."

"Lovely." Then he frowned. The idea of his usual large portion of cottage pie was very tempting, but . . .

"Not too much for me, please. I'm an athlete in training, remember."

Heather looked a little uncertain.

"Are you sure that's not taking things a bit far?"

He shook his head and smiled.

"I need to be in top condition for this race."

They had barely picked up their knives and forks when the phone rang.

"That was Keira," Heather explained, her face pale as she replaced the receiver. "She's having contractions. Frank wants to take her to hospital, but she won't go because there's nobody to look after Jenny."

Martin frowned. Heather's sister wasn't due to have her second baby for another two months.

"Of course – your mum and dad are away this week, aren't they?"

"She was wondering if I could drive up now," Heather said, frowning, looking from Martin to her son.

"Of course you must go," Martin insisted. "We'll be fine, won't we, Robbie?"

Robbie didn't look at all certain, but he nodded nonetheless and earned grateful smiles from his mother and stepfather.

Heather left immediately, without even finishing her meal. By the time Martin and Robbie had eaten, tidied everything away and Robbie had done his homework, it was time for the boy to go to bed.

Martin congratulated himself on an evening successfully negotiated. Not that he had expected Robbie to be any trouble – the child's manners were faultless. But things could sometimes be a bit awkward between the two of them, what with Robbie's reluctance to chat to him.

THE morning routine meant there was, again, little time for any awkward silences. They hurriedly got ready, and Martin poured out two bowls of cereal while simultaneously speaking to Heather on the phone.

"No news yet," she confirmed. "Last I heard they were trying to stop the contractions. I'm just waiting to hear from Frank."

She had a quick word with Robbie that left him with a smile on his face, and then, after Martin hurriedly called his office to let everyone know he would be late, it was time to leave.

Luckily he was his own boss, so there wasn't much anyone could say, but he was glad he had a good excuse nonetheless. Especially as he would have to leave early this afternoon. And no excuse could be as good as caring for Robbie.

After school they went out for tea to Robbie's favourite pizza restaurant.

He ordered a salad for himself; he hadn't been joking when he'd told Heather he wanted to get fit. Robbie seemed happy enough to order his usual pizza.

"Your mum says Auntie Keira still hasn't had her baby," he explained, pausing while the waiter brought their drinks. "But Gran and Grandpa will be back in a few days, so Mum will be home by the weekend."

Robbie nodded, picked up his lemonade and took a sip. Martin suppressed a heartfelt sigh.

"You know your mum's been helping me to train for this race?" he ventured after a minute.

Robbie nodded again.

"Well . . ." Martin faltered. This might go badly. But all he could do was ask.

"I'd really appreciate it if you could record my times while she's away. Do you think you could come down to the track with me and take charge of the stopwatch?"

He saw a spark of interest in Robbie's expression and held his breath.

"OK," the boy agreed, and Martin let his breath out. It was a start.

Heather had been right. With a shared interest, conversation was suddenly much easier, and over the next few nights, down at the track, Martin even dared to hope he might have bonded with his stepson.

"That was terrible!" Robbie laughed as Martin finished his latest lap.

Martin couldn't answer right away – he was too out of breath. It didn't feel as though he was getting any better at this. But he did manage a wide and genuine grin through his panting. It was nice to see Robbie laughing, even if it was at him.

"Still six weeks of training to go before the big day," he managed eventually. "I'm bound to improve if I keep trying."

Robbie said nothing, and Martin was grateful for his tact.

"They managed to stop the contractions, but they're keeping her in," Heather explained when she got back. She looked pale and worried, and Martin took her in his arms and gave her a reassuring cuddle.

"It's best she's in hospital, where they can keep an eye on her and the baby." She nodded.

"How did it go with Robbie?"

"OK, I think." But to his utter delight, Martin realised his reply had been overcautious when the boy joined them a few minutes later.

"You don't need to go down to the track with Martin tonight, Mum," Robbie told her. "I'm recording his times now. It'll give you a chance to have a break."

Martin and Heather exchanged smiles over Robbie's head. This was progress!

As the weeks passed, getting around the track proved no easier. But Martin enjoyed his growing camaraderie at the track with his stepson. The effect was continued at home.

"Can you help me with this maths homework, please, Martin?" Robbie asked one night.

"Of course," Martin agreed gladly. "Bring your books and we'll work on the dining table."

"Thanks." Robbie smiled, and Martin thought it was moments like this that made the torture of training after work each evening just about bearable.

Keira's second little girl was born the night before the race.

"Mother and baby are both doing well," Heather reported. "They're all wishing you the best of luck for tomorrow."

"Great." Martin beamed, pleased the baby had arrived safely, but also grateful for the good wishes for the race. His time was still not brilliant. He would need all the luck he could get.

HE didn't win, not even nearly. But he wasn't last, either, and that was good enough for him. There were two competitors slower than him, so he wasn't completely disgraced.

"You did brilliantly," Heather told him as he joined his family.

He grinned, quietly proud of his achievement.

"All right for an old bloke, eh?" he asked Robbie.

"Not bad," Robbie agreed. "Next year, you can start training sooner. Maybe we could run together."

He knew there was still a long way to go, but this was a better reaction than Martin had ever dared hope for.

It had taken months of hard work – and the effort had nearly killed him. But there was no doubt that running in the dads' race at Robbie's school was the best thing he had ever done. He felt like he'd won gold. ∎

Holly's Harvest

By Amanda Brittany.

O UR next-door neighbour, Mr Blake, was an awkward customer to say the least. He was extremely set in his ways, having been a widower for more than ten years. And if he wasn't taking issue with the branches of our tree hanging into his garden, or the smell of our barbecue wafting over his fence, he was finding something else to complain about.

But my young daughter Holly seemed to like him, and would always throw him one of her beaming smiles as we passed his house on our way to school, clearly seeing something in him I struggled to see myself.

"Hello, Mr Blake," she said the other morning, forcing him to return her small wave as he turned towards his house, muttering to himself. And as he closed his door, she looked up at me and said, "I feel a bit sorry for him, Mummy. Hardly anyone goes to see him."

Thankfully I refrained from saying I wasn't at all surprised. As we walked in the sunshine that day, Holly looked up at me with bright eyes.

"Do you think I could help Mr Blake on his allotment to get my Brownie Gardener Badge?" she asked, and I admit it was on the tip of my tongue to say no. But

86

her enthusiasm was such that I nodded, despite my reservations.

"Of course, darling," I said, trying to hide my uncertainty. And when we arrived at Mr Blake's small patch of earth a few days later, my daughter clasping her small, flowery bag of gardening tools, I became even more convinced I was making a mistake.

"Good morning, Mr Blake," Holly said with a big smile, and he paused from digging and looked over at us.

"We've got a lovely day for it," I said, feeling a little apprehensive.

"Too hot, if you ask me," he said, taking a handkerchief from his pocket and dabbing his forehead, his eyes falling on Holly.

"You're a tiny thing," he went on, as she looked around her, eyes sparkling. And I admit her arms did look rather small poking from the sleeves of her T-shirt.

"She's stronger than she looks, aren't you, darling?" I said, crouching and cupping her shoulders, and she nodded.

"Well, I'm not sure a wee thing like you is going to be much help here," he continued, plunging his fork into the dry soil and pausing to catch his breath.

"I will be," Holly said, thrusting her hands on her hips, and tossing her dark curls. "I'm not a Sixer of the Pixies for nothing, you know. Look at all of these, Mr Blake," she added, pointing at the brightly coloured array of badges I'd lovingly sewn on to her uniform over the past year, but he didn't look her way.

"She can swim," I chipped in, quickly wishing I hadn't.

"Well, there's not much call for swimmers on an allotment."

"I've got a healthy heart," Holly said undeterred. "I'm a collector and a good communicator."

"Are you now?" Mr Blake said finally, his bushy grey eyebrows meeting in the middle as he put down his spade. He flopped in his deckchair and grabbed his newspaper, holding it up as if wanting something to hide behind. "Well, if you're a good communicator, lass, you'll know it's time to stop talking and start weeding," he concluded, pointing at a little a patch of weeds.

"I think I'll stay," I muttered, pulling up another deckchair and taking a book from my bag, deciding I ought to stick around in case things ended in tears.

"You don't have to stay, Mummy," Holly said, dropping to her knees and picking up her trowel. "I'm quite capable, you know."

"I know you are, sweetheart. Just pretend I'm not here," I said, trying for a smile, which Mr Blake didn't return.

AS I sat in the sunshine I realised that, although Mr Blake had made a fine job of growing rows of vegetables, and his rhubarb leaves waved gently in the breeze like giant hands, the allotment was alive with weeds. In fact, it appeared he'd done little work there lately.

After weeding for some time, Holly tugged at Mr Blake's newspaper and I stopped pretending to read my book.

"Guess what other badges I've got?" she said, smiling once more.

"What you need, my girl," he said, "is an 'I-know-when-to-be-quiet' badge."

I shuffled, trying not to lose my patience, but Holly said, biting her lip, "I don't actually think they do one of those, do they, Mummy?"

I shook my head, glimpsing a small smile on Mr Blake's lips.

"No, they don't," I said pointedly.

"Would you like me to dig up some more weeds for you?" Holly continued.

Mr Blake folded his paper, rose to his feet, and showed her another patch.

"Now be careful with these ones, Holly," he said. "You might pull up the vegetables by mistake. Have you heard 'The Tale Of Peter Rabbit'?"

"I have," Holly said with a laugh, and Mr Blake laughed, too, although his resemblance to Mr McGregor was a little too uncanny.

"Why do we have to keep the weeds away?" she asked eventually, a pile of dandelions by her side. I was eager to help, but fidgeted my deckchair into a patch of shade instead, not wanting to interfere.

"Because they might tangle round the vegetables and stop them growing," Mr Blake explained.

"Grumpy old weeds," Holly said with a laugh, and I smiled.

"Grumpy old weeds have their place sometimes," he said gruffly. "They're not all bad. Do you know, flowering ones attract the bees."

"So happy weeds are OK."

"If you say so," he said, ruffling her head with genuine affection.

It was a pleasure to watch them lapse into chatter as they worked together,

Smoo Cave

A NATURAL sea cave, Smoo Cave is situated one mile to the east of Durness village centre. The approach to the cave is very impressive, with an entrance 50 feet high, 130 feet wide and 200 feet long. Inside the cave you will find a covered wooden pathway and bridge that takes you to a magnificent cascade that falls into a deep pool.

Boat trips into the cave last 20 minutes and operate in April, May, June, July, August and September, but please check times before you go as they do vary and all trips are weather dependent. It might also be an idea to pack a pair of walking boots, as the cave is only accessible via a rough path from the car park. However, the cave is open all year round and admission is free.

weeding and digging. Mr Blake told Holly that he was once a Boy Scout.

"Dib, dib, dob," he said, doing the sign with his fingers, and she giggled.

"I'm off to Betty's Café for a fry-up," Mr Blake said at lunchtime, and I realised my stomach was rumbling.

"That's not particularly good for you." Holly's face grew serious. "We've got salad sandwiches. Would you like one?"

"Well, I don't mind if I do," he said, and she handed one over. As they ate, he pointed out and named butterflies and birds, and Holly was enthralled, her eyes wide. She'd got her heart set on the Wildlife Explorer badge, too. In fact, there wasn't a badge she didn't want to try for.

At the end of the afternoon, I felt like I'd learned a lot, too, and Mr Blake cut some rhubarb and bagged vegetables for us to take home.

"My late wife used to cook lovely crumbles," he said, lowering his head to disguise a shimmer in his eyes, and I sensed his grumpy exterior was a cover for how much he still missed her. "But I'm not one for cooking anything fancy, and far too long in the tooth to learn," he added.

That evening Holly, with her usual rush of enthusiasm, decided she'd like to try for the cook badge.

"Make a healthy dish showing you can prepare fresh fruits, vegetables or salad. Arrange it in an appetising way," she read, smiling up at me pleadingly.

"OK," I said, and we gathered together all the necessary ingredients.

WHEN we arrived at the allotment the following day, Mr Blake was sitting in his deckchair, a checked hat pulled over his face, his cardigan buttoned thoroughly.

"Hello," Holly said. "Guess what? I've made you something."

He pulled off his hat and dragged himself upright, and I couldn't help noticing a spark of interest in his eyes.

"Have you, young lady?" he said.

"It's a rhubarb crumble, made with wholemeal flour. It had to be healthy, to earn my Brownie badge."

Mr Blake took it with open arms.

"You deserve it," he said. "This will be lovely with a nice bit of custard."

"Low fat," Holly insisted.

"Why don't you come round for dinner?" I asked, surprising myself, and Holly smiled up at me. "Perhaps one day next week?"

"Thank you, I'd like that very much."

"And I'll teach you how to cook things that are good for you, if you'd like," Holly said. "We could use some of your lovely vegetables."

"We could indeed," he said, beaming. "What a kind girl you are."

I looked from his twinkling eyes to my daughter's delighted face, and smiled proudly. If only there was a badge for winning over Mr Blake, I thought.

Holly would have earned it hands down. ■

by Sheila Aird.

Getting Away From It All

Illustration by Ruth Blair.

IWAS just ten years old when we went on holiday to Dunsford for the first time. Being a head teacher, my dad always looked forward to "getting away from it all" during his long summer break. In February of that year, when one of his colleagues mentioned that Dunsford was the ideal place to unwind, a family paradise, in fact, well – that was it, really.

Mum sacrificed her dreams of a holiday in Tuscany and made enquiries about self-catering accommodation in the small seaside town on the south coast. She ended up booking Miss Evadne Shelldrake's cottage above Petticoat Bay for the month of August.

I loved Bayview Cottage.

It was up a winding lane just off the main road, a cosy, semi-detached cottage with a living-room and a huge kitchen downstairs, and a bathroom

91

and two bedrooms with sloping roofs in the attic. Even now, years later, I can still remember my bedroom with its pine furniture, white wicker chairs and worn blue carpet. The bed was so big that climbing into it each night was like conquering a mountain.

As for Miss Shelldrake, she lived in the next-door cottage. She was, from my ten-year-old point of view, quite different from any other grown-up. From the beginning she said we were all to call her Evadne.

"Everyone does." She beamed as she took the key to the cottage from under a flowerpot outside the front door. "Here we are, then. I've left a bowl of eggs on the kitchen table. If there's anything you need I'm just next door – except between nine o'clock and one o'clock." She turned to me. "I work in the village shop, Pippa. We sell everything from pasta to postcards."

E VADNE was small and round with golden skin and the palest of blue eyes. Her thick brown hair was piled on top of her head and secured discreetly with two short, thick wooden knitting needles.

At the time I didn't think wearing knitting needles was in the least strange. Nor can I remember wondering why Evadne wore earrings with clown faces. I held her gaze.

"Do you sell fishing nets?" I asked solemnly.

"Of course." She was equally serious. "We've got several different colours – green, blue, white and orange. They're selling fast. Would you like me to keep one for you?"

I nodded.

"A blue one, please. It's my favourite colour."

"What a coincidence." Evadne's eyes widened in pleased surprise. "It's my favourite, too."

Somehow, having that one simple thing in common created a bond between us.

On the third morning of our holiday I woke quite early to the sound of Evadne talking to someone.

"Come on then, you silly girls – that's it. No – shoo! SHOO –"

I got up and pulled back the curtains. Then I caught my breath in surprise. Evadne was talking to her chickens. Suddenly she looked up and gave a cheerful wave. I pushed open the window and waved back.

"Good morning, Pippa. Isn't it a lovely day? Come and help me feed the girls."

I dressed quickly and ran down.

The chickens lived in a coop in the small orchard beyond the garden at the back of the cottages. They had their own fenced area where they roamed quite happily.

"Here you are, take this bowl of corn. They'll do the rest."

I did as I was told – reluctantly.

"Do they bite?" I asked as they pecked at the food I'd thrown.

"No, not at all. They're lovely girls."

"What are their names?"

"That one is called Twinkle, that's Bonnie, this one's Trudy –"

"They're amazing," I whispered, suddenly fascinated by the whole exercise.

THAT month in Dunsford it hardly rained. Before breakfast, I'd help Evadne to feed the chickens. Then I'd wander up the grassy path through the orchard.

From the top of the slope I could see the full curve of the bay with its sandy beach and a row of colourful beach huts. The sea was a flat, dark mass. It went on for ever until it disappeared under the sky.

Dunsford suited all of us. Dad spent long, sunlit days on the beach, dozing in his deckchair or doing a crossword, while Mum read countless paperbacks and allowed the sun to turn her skin a pale golden colour.

As for me, I played with other children. We pottered about at the edge of the waves or built sandcastles that disappeared when the tide came in.

One afternoon, armed with my blue fishing net, I searched the rocky pools under the cliffs for sea creatures and took them back to the cottage in a jam jar to show Evadne.

"So what do you think?" I said, pouring the contents of the jar into a washing-up bowl on the grass. As the sand dispersed and sank to the bottom, tiny creatures moved lazily around in the clear water. "Do you know what they're called?" I asked Evadne.

"I'm not sure. I'll get my encyclopaedia."

There was a whole page of information on sea-life.

"That one looks like a lugworm," Evadne said, pointing to a long, thin creature. "And that one is definitely a shrimp."

"And that one's a crab," I said, stirring the water gently with a twig. "Isn't he tiny?"

"They're all quite small, Pippa. They would have been washed in by the tide. They could have come from anywhere, France, maybe, or even Spain."

We spent ages trying to identify the creatures in the washing-up bowl until the light began to fade.

"What should I do with them now?"

She frowned thoughtfully.

"You could put them back in the jar and take them back to their little pool. Maybe the next tide will wash them back home."

It was the obvious thing to do.

One evening Evadne looked after me while Mum and Dad went to the Dunsford Pavilion to see a play.

"It'll be nice having company for tea," she said. "Sausages, beans and chips all right with you, Pippa ?"

It was my favourite food. I nodded.

Evadne's own cottage was a mirror-image of the one we were staying in, only shabbier. Her living-room was cluttered with weird objects. Funny-looking vases, photographs in frames, loads of tiny boxes – they all jostled for space on different surfaces. But the room was dominated by a large bookcase.

"You've got lots of books," I said, peering at the titles.

"The ones on that shelf are all about travel. I love reading about other countries."

"What's that?" I asked, moving to the table in the bay window.

"It's a telescope. It belonged to my grandfather. Have a look through it, if you want."

I pressed my eye up against the glass and stared through the lens.

"I can't see anything," I said. "Just the sea and a straight line and the sky."

Evadne laughed.

"That straight line is called the horizon. Actually, there's a huge space between the sea and the sky. If you could fly across the sea you'd reach France."

"How long would it take?"

"Oh, ages. It's a beautiful country." Her pale eyes lit up with enthusiasm. "The biggest city in France is called Paris. Shall I tell you about Paris?"

For the next hour or so I was transfixed. First, Evadne produced a map of France and we pinpointed Paris. Then she described the city in such loving detail that I felt as if I was there: the Eiffel Tower, Notre Dame, the Louvre – I

Thinkstockphotos.

Rainbow Of Flowers

IT is blissfully quiet
In our garden today,
Where scented flowers bloom
And some snowy doves play.

Under milky-blue skies
There's a quiet summer heat,
Below tall, shady trees
We've a soft, comfy seat.

Songbirds are trilling
Sweet notes of thanksgiving,
With honeybees humming
For the sweet joy of living!

With a soft cloud of butterflies
Floating above,
We've a rainbow of flowers
In a garden of love!

– Maggie Smith.

could almost see them . . .

"You'll go to Paris one day and see it all for yourself," she finished. "Now, let's have some drinking chocolate before your parents come to collect you."

I followed her into the kitchen.

"Have you been to a lot of countries, Evadne?"

"I haven't actually been anywhere, Pippa." She sighed. "When I was young, we didn't have much money so we spent our holidays here at home. Then I grew up and I had responsibilities."

"What kind of responsibilities?"

"Well." She spooned drinking chocolate into two mugs. "My mother died so I had to look after my father and our cottage next door. I helped Dad with the chickens and I had my job in the village shop, too, so I was always busy. Now that I'm on my own, I have even more responsibilities. Maybe one day . . ."

"I see." I thought for a moment. "Still, you've got your lovely books."

"Yes, yes I have. And they're filled with all kinds of information so I feel as if I've been everywhere. Of course, it's not the same."

"Next time, will you tell me about some of the other places you haven't been?"

Evadne smiled.

"If you like."

Mum once commented that Dunsford was the seaside town that time forgot; it was stuck in the nineteen-fifties. On reflection, I think she was right. Yet we kept going back. There was something magical about the cottage above the bay, and as the years marched past in regimented blocks of school terms, I always looked forward to spending August in Dunsford.

I OFTEN wrote to Evadne. My letters were filled with useless information about what was happening in my life. She shared the drama when I fell out with my best friend. She commiserated when I wasn't chosen for the netball team. And she was the first to know when I passed a music exam.

Sometimes I'd enclose a drawing or a cutting from a magazine that I thought might interest her. I always sent love to the chickens and hoped they'd remember me when I saw them in August.

Evadne used to reply by return. Her letters were usually three or four pages long and beautifully printed so that they were easy to read. She'd comment on my news and keep me up to date with what was happening in Dunsford, and about her latest travel book.

At some point during each holiday, Mum and Dad would go to the theatre or out for a meal and I'd spend the evening with Evadne. We'd get out her big map and several travel books and we'd choose a country to focus on.

Evadne's enthusiasm was so infectious it was a lovely, effortless way to learn. It made me realise that we lived in a beautiful world.

We rented the cottage six years running. Then Mum suggested that we could go somewhere different for a change.

"There isn't much for a teenager to do in Dunsford," she said, pointing out the obvious. "Maybe we should be thinking about that holiday in Tuscany."

"But I love Dunsford," I protested. "And I love our cottage – and the chickens. I can always find someone to play tennis with and now that the swimming pool has reopened –" I ran out of reasons.

Mum looked at Dad.

"You know what I think, love." He grinned.

"Seems I'm outnumbered – again," Mum said. "I'll phone Evadne."

* * * *

When we arrived, Evadne came out to meet us as usual. I couldn't get out the car quick enough to give her a big hug.

"How are the chickens? Did Trudy recover?"

"She's fine. She's fine, Pippa." Evadne laughed and her eyes crinkled into tiny slits. "I've left a bowl of fresh eggs on the kitchen table as usual. Now, let me look at you. My, how you've grown. You must be four inches taller than me."

"Three and a half." I giggled. "I'm the tallest in my class."

While Mum and Dad unpacked the car, Evadne and I went into the orchard to check on the chickens.

"I told them you were coming," she said as we leaned over the wire fence and watched the chickens pecking away at non-existent food.

A gentle wind danced through the trees, making them sway to the sound of

96

the sea. Happiness washed over me.

"It's so peaceful here." I sighed. "I'd never want to go anywhere else for my holidays."

"Of course you would, Pippa." Evadne's voice was gentle. "You're sixteen. Dunsford will be 'old hat' sooner than you think."

"What about you, Evadne? You never take a holiday. Don't you want to go to some of the places you've told me about?"

"Oh, yes. It would be wonderful. But I have the girls to think about." She cooed to the chickens. "They need looking after. Then there's the cottage and my job . . ." She looked at me and her expression was grave. "Still too many responsibilities, I'm afraid."

"But what if you didn't have any responsibilities?" I persisted. "Where would you go?"

She didn't even hesitate.

"I'd go to Paris." She sighed wistfully. "Yes. I want to see Paris."

After that we went back to Dunsford twice more. Despite Mum's fears that I would be bored, I never was. When I wasn't playing tennis, or swimming, or meeting people I'd made friends with over the years, I'd spend my time dipping into Evadne's travel books.

Then, just as Evadne had predicted, everything changed.

THE year Mum and Dad celebrated their twentieth wedding anniversary they decided to do something special.

I was surprised when Mum announced where they were going.

"South America, Pippa." Her eyes were like diamonds. "Dad's taking me to South America. We'll leave at the end of July and be away for the school holidays."

Suddenly she looked anxious.

"You'll be all right on your own, won't you, pet?"

"Of course I will." I laughed. At eighteen I was perfectly happy to stay on my own. I'd get a summer job and earn enough money to have a holiday with friends before I started my arts course at university that October.

"I'll phone Evadne. Let her know what's happening."

Evadne was thrilled to hear about the trip.

"But what about you, Pippa? You're welcome to come and stay with me while your parents are away. I'd love to have you. I'm sure you'd find a summer job in one of the cafés."

It was an offer I couldn't refuse.

I found a job in a gift shop on the prom. Evadne and I settled into a neat routine. We'd cook dinner together and, after we'd washed up, we'd take our coffee into the garden and watch the sun going down.

When it rained, as it did several times, we watched television or played board games. Most evenings we'd end up opening at least one travel book.

We had long discussions about life in general and what I wanted to do when I got my degree. The summer flew past.

When I said goodbye to Evadne at the end of August, she gave me an exquisite little antique brooch, shaped like a crab and studded with tiny diamonds.

"To remind you of Dunsford," she whispered, blinking back her tears.

"Oh, Evadne, it's beautiful. Thank you so much."

We hugged each other tight.

"Dunsford will always be my favourite place," I whispered fiercely. "I'll see you next August as usual."

Evadne just nodded. That was the last time I saw her.

THAT October I went to Edinburgh University and became caught up in student life from the start. I lived in halls for the first year and that's how I met Harriet and Holly, my two best friends.

From the second year onwards we shared a flat together: the three musketeers! We all had the travel bug so vacations were spent travelling around different countries, and working in them when we could. France, America, Thailand – life was hectic and fun.

Even so, I always kept in touch with Evadne and she with me.

I sent her letters and postcards and keepsakes from foreign cities. I took dozens of photographs of unusual views and beautiful buildings and narrow streets off the beaten track and sent them to her with my love.

Several months after I graduated, I landed my ideal job in a fine art gallery here in Paris.

That was more than a year ago.

Now I rent a one-bedroom apartment with a view over the rooftops. There's hardly enough room to turn in the tiny kitchen and I've bumped my head on the low ceiling in the bathroom a thousand times. But there's a sofa-bed in the living-room and a special guest is arriving today.

Evadne is coming to stay. I'm on my way to the airport to meet her.

Now she's retired, she has one less responsibility so I decided it was time to make her first dream come true.

Mum and Dad have taken the cottage, as usual. Mum has promised to look after "the girls" and Dad will keep an eye on Evadne's cottage and tend her garden.

As the coach nears the airport, I begin to feel excited. I can hardly wait to see Evadne again. For the next two weeks we'll be tourists. We'll visit all the places Evadne has longed to see: the Eiffel Tower, the Louvre, Notre Dame, the Arc de Triomphe and the rest. They're all familiar to me. But I'll be seeing them through her eyes, just like I did all those years ago when she brought them to life from the pages of that book.

I glance at the crab brooch pinned to my lapel and touch the catch to make sure it's secure. Then I smile. As always, the brooch reminds me of blue fishing nets and rock pools . . . and Dunsford, where it all began. ■

Fifty Years Ago . . .

August 12, 1964

RENOWNED author Ian Fleming died, leaving behind a rich legacy of books which are still being enjoyed 50 years on. He is undoubtedly best known for his novels featuring the suave and sophisticated James Bond.

The 007 agent is just as popular – perhaps even more so – than he was in the 60s. He has been portrayed several times on TV and film, with the best-known film portrayals coming from seven actors – David Niven, Sean Connery, George Lazenby, Roger Moore, Timothy Dalton, Pierce Brosnan and Daniel Craig. It is said that many of the spy's likes, dislikes and traits were reflections of the author. Visually he resembled Ian Fleming, too.

Fleming also created one of the best-loved children's books of all time – "Chitty, Chitty Bang Bang" – which was to go on to be immortalised in film with Dick Van Dyke playing the lead role. Over the last few years it has enjoyed success as a stage musical, too. ■

JAMES BOND
From Russia with Love
A classic Bond adventure
IAN FLEMING

PA Images.

PA Images.

All That Jazz

by John Kenworthy.

T HEY had a new vicar at St Aidan's. The Reverend Roland (Roly) Fitzwilliam was young and progressive and rode round his parish on a bicycle with dropped handlebars. He had already introduced several new hymn tunes that some of the choir considered a little too secular. Whilst not veering as far towards blasphemy as this new "rock 'n' roll" stuff, some of these new tunes would not have sounded out of place on "The Light Programme".

Miss Warrington, who had played the organ and taken choir practice for the last 30 years, was shocked to be asked if she could find something a bit more zippy than Stainer or Parry.

"Let's have some hymns you can snap your fingers to," Roly suggested.

Miss Warrington furrowed her brow with dismay. Isaac Watts, she felt, would have turned in his grave.

The familiar, comfortable and sonorous cadences of the Authorised Version were abandoned, and something simpler, more comprehensible but less magical, put in their place. Prayers were brisker. The new vicar's sermons were – well, chatty!

To some of the congregation, it seemed that awe and majesty were taking a back seat and glory was watered down.

"The Lord," Miss Warrington grumbled to Miss Hathaway, "seems more like some kind of Managing Director than Our Father in Heaven."

There were, it would be fair to say, murmurings of discontent in the front pews.

These came to a head over the St George's Day Fête.

As long as anyone could remember, the smallish lawn behind St Aidan's had been home to the modest marquee erected for the occasion.

Inside the marquee there was always a cake and pastry stall bearing Miss Warrington's rock cakes, Mrs Baldwin's scones, Miss Hathaway's blackberry

Illustration by Patricia Ludlow.

100

and apple pie, Mrs Stott's coconut macaroons, and a range
of differently iced fairy cakes from other members of the
congregation. Somebody usually contributed a Victoria
sponge, too.

At the other side of the marquee stood the produce stall,
stocked largely from Mr Gibson's allotment and consisting of
rather slender carrots, leggy spring greens, and more brussels
sprouts than anyone could possibly eat. Not to mention early Cheshire
potatoes. There were usually some of Mr Fancourt-Browne's hothouse-grown
tomatoes, ready for their buyers to ripen on their own window-sills.

A refreshment stand where it was possible to purchase plenty of
Mrs Backhouse's home-made lemonade, rationed portions (one glass per

customer) of Mr Chatterton's elderflower wine, or unlimited plastic cups of tea from the parish urn, stood further back.

Also set up in the marquee was a handicrafts stall with a collection of crocheted doilies, woolly bobble-hats with matching mittens, jars of bath salts, fringed place-mats, hand-decorated plant-pot holders, tea cosies, bed socks, tie-dyed T-shirts and wooden plaques bearing the instruction *Bless This House*.

AFTER a tea provided by the ladies of the parish, and a short address from the vicar thanking everyone who had helped make this such a special event, all those attending would adjourn to St Aidan's Church Hall for a talk and a slide show delivered by a church member. Once the vicar had complimented Mr Baldwin (say) on the quality of his transparencies of Stonehenge (say), everyone could go home in the warm glow of knowing they had done their bit.

The St George's Day Fête was a cosy tradition whose very familiarity reassured St Aidan's parishioners that all was well with their world.

The Reverend Roly Fitzwilliam soon put a stop to that.

He insulted the Fête Committee – describing them as unchanged since the French Revolution – by suggesting some younger blood.

He hired a bigger marquee and invited the local fire brigade, St John's Ambulance, the Boy Scouts and Civic Trust to take part for starters, which sounded ominous.

There would be an address from a representative of the Neighbourhood Watch in the marquee, and a policeman would be present!

"We'll make it a true community event," he told the astonished committee. "Do something to really put St Aidan's on the map."

Before Mr Gibson, the verger, could properly open his mouth, Roly added, "And, in the evening, we'll have a dance."

"But . . ." Mr Gibson managed.

"You don't have to worry about a band," the Reverend said. "My brother plays in one."

It was not until the posters went up that St Aidan's horrified congregation realised what it had let itself in for, or the extent of the humiliation it was to endure.

The dancers in the church hall were not to be accompanied by select instrumentalists from the Walter Hargreaves Ballroom Orchestra, the established and respectable organisation that traditionally added sedate syncopation to Masonic and Rotary functions, but by the New Orleans Chilli Peppers – a hot jazz septet from Reigate.

Even Miss Hathaway's discovery that the clarinet player was a clerk at her local bank did nothing to soften the blow.

It was all presented to the Church Council as a *fait accompli*; their renegade vicar even smiled broadly at them as he announced what, to the

102

elders of his flock, amounted almost to apostasy.

Reverend Fitzwilliam noticed the wide eyes and open mouths in his audience, and smiled happily.

"I think I've made quite an impression," he told his wife at teatime.

MISS HATHAWAY and Mr Gibson arranged a secret meeting in Alice's Tea Rooms in Rayne's Park, to discuss and, if possible, determine a strategy to deal with the assault on their cherished traditions.

It was unlike Miss Hathaway to be heading up a die-hard revolt. She was – as she would readily have explained to anyone – of a generally easy-going and tolerant disposition, not a boat-rocker of any sort. Nor was she opposed to change, as her recent purchase of colourful wellies for her gardening amply demonstrated.

But she did not like the sacred rituals of her worship being tampered with without so much as a by-your-leave, nor did she approve of people who were not members of St Aidan's congregation, or even residents of Aspen Avenue, being casually invited into her life.

She knew nothing about the Civic Trust, but the very name suggested to her an organisation that might be a bit interfering. And she thought the mere mention of the Neighbourhood Watch would concentrate the wrong sort of attention on the district. If burglars thought there was something worth watching, it might give them ideas.

Then there was the jazz.

"We have to take a stand somewhere," Mr Gibson said. "If we don't, we might finish up anywhere; people playing guitars in church – that sort of thing."

"Heavens!" Miss Hathaway exclaimed.

"Hell, more likely," Mr Gibson said glumly. "We don't want those Devil's instruments in St Aidan's, do we?"

"I suppose not," Miss Hathaway replied, uncertain as to why violins, for instance, could be heavenly, and another stringed instrument unholy. But Mr Gibson was ecumenically better informed than her, so she accepted his assessment.

"What do you suggest we do?" she asked, not for the first time.

"We could demonstrate. Isn't that what they do these days? Outside the vicarage would be a good place."

"You mean waving placards and things?" Miss Hathaway was aghast. "But people would see us."

"That's the point of demonstrations." Mr Gibson was in militant mode, brandishing a teaspoon. "Stand up and be counted, that's what I say."

"Don't you think that's rather extreme?" Miss Hathaway queried.

"Extreme measures demand extreme responses," Mr Gibson replied – in his mind's eye he carried a crusader's banner. "We have a fight ahead. We

must take arms."

"Wouldn't it be easier to get a deputation together to put our point of view across to the vicar?"

"I feel we should do something more positive than that." Mr Gibson had the light of battle in his eyes. "We must not take it lying down."

"I'm not suggesting we do take it that way," Miss Hathaway said, unhappy with the metaphor. "But should we not try persuasion before force?"

Though both Miss Hathaway and Mr Gibson agreed that something should be done, they were in apparently irreconcilable disagreement as to what that something should be, and how it should be achieved. They decided to invite Mrs Stott along to their next meeting to listen to their arguments and arbitrate between them.

CIVIL disobedience might work," Mrs Stott agreed.

"What's civil disobedience?" Miss Hathaway and Mr Gibson asked in unison.

"Not quite sure," Mrs Stott admitted. "I think it's a bit like sitting down in the middle of the road."

"That's just plain silly," Mr Gibson said. "If you sat down in Oaklands Road, you'd be run over in seconds."

"You could sit on the zebra crossing," Miss Hathaway put in.

"I didn't mean literally. Just as an example," Mrs Stott explained. "I meant something more like when the vicar says 'Will the congregation please rise?' we all stay seated. Or, if he tells us to kneel for prayers, we all stand up."

"I don't think that's very polite," Miss Hathaway observed.

104

Dawdling

IT'S the kind of day for dawdling,
The sun is shining bright,
Everything is blissful,
A truly marvellous sight.
The birds are trilling 'mongst the leaves,
Their pure sweet notes entrance,
There is a magic in the air
That can't be there by chance.
Sheep are grazing in the fields
And wander at their ease,
As the gentle summer's breath
Caresses willow trees.
So now I will take my leave
And dawdle on my way,
To revel in the wonder
Of this tranquil summer's day . . .

– Brian H. Gent.

"I don't think it would work." Mr Gibson frowned.

"It worked all right for Gandhi," Mrs Stott said.

"Who's Gandhi?" Miss Hathaway asked.

They decided to see what Mr Chatterton had to say, and he thought they ought to write to the Bishop.

More St Aidan's churchgoers were consulted.

AFTER several months of polite and genteel wrangling, they were still no nearer to deciding on a course of action. But it didn't really matter. In the meantime, the fête took place.

It was, as Mr Gibson grudgingly admitted, an unqualified success.

The vicar had – entirely without asking anyone – found a brass band from somewhere, whose bold music drew visitors off the streets to be piously fleeced at the refreshments stall. For the first time in the fête's history, they ran out of jam tarts.

The various local societies on display made generous contributions to Church and Circuit Funds. Mr Fancourt-Browne sold all his tomatoes!

The Jazz Band Ball in the evening was, in Mr Chatterton's phrase, "a real wow!", and Miss Hathaway, to everyone's surprise – not least her own – danced an energetic Charleston with Mr Baldwin.

There were people there from as far afield as Leatherhead, and, for the first time in living memory, the event made a profit that ran well into three figures.

Shortly after the fête, the Conservation Committee – as they had begun to call themselves – called an urgent meeting, and decided unanimously to disband. ■

A Leap Of Faith

THE wind whipped at the hem of Lucy's skirt as she leaned against the promenade rail and looked down at the deserted beach below. Shivering, she wondered again why she had ever thought that coming here was a good idea.

At the water's edge, a man in a long raincoat was picking his way cautiously over the pebbles and trying to dodge the incoming waves. A lead dangled loosely from his hand as a bedraggled collie ran on ahead, stopping every now and then to push its nose into a rock pool, its tail wagging furiously with excitement.

Lucy scraped back the stray locks of damp windswept hair that kept flapping at her face and gazed out across the whole length of the beach.

There was nobody else, just a few scraps of litter bouncing haphazardly along the sand, and the occasional bird.

Well, it wasn't really surprising, she thought. No-one else would be stupid enough to come to the seaside on a day like this.

She pulled the collar of her coat up more tightly around her neck and struggled to control her wayward skirt as it threatened to lift in the wind. But, of course, it didn't really matter if it did. There was nobody around to see.

The seaside in autumn was nothing like the jolly, bustling place she remembered from the last time she'd been here, with Dan. Now it just seemed lonely and deserted, reflecting the way she'd been feeling, too, these last few days.

She had come here on a whim; just grabbed the bare essentials and bought a coach ticket, with no real plan other than to get away.

Somewhere in the back of her mind was the wish to recapture some of the magic she had felt on that other day, two summers ago, when they had both just graduated from universities at opposite ends of the country, and she and her twin had stood on this very spot, without a care in the world, watching the waves, happy just to be together again after three hectic years apart.

The sun had shone brightly then, and the beach had been bustling with holidaymakers. But that was before Dan's accident. Before that terrible motorbike crash that had changed everything.

Illustration by John Hancock.

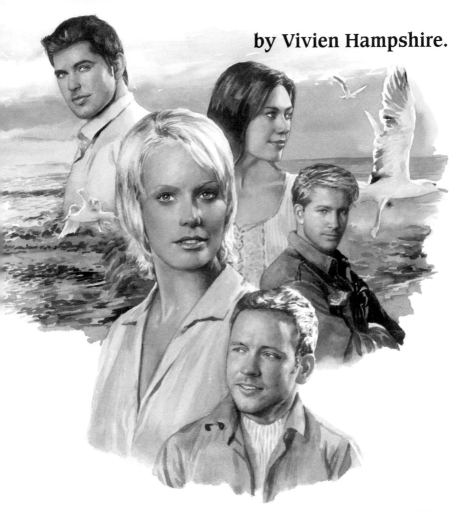

by Vivien Hampshire.

Now there was no sunshine, no crowds, and whatever magic she had felt then had most definitely gone.

SHE couldn't help thinking that coming back here might have been a mistake. Dan was miles away, trying to do something he had always wanted to do, and insistent that he could – and would – manage it without her help.

"You're stifling me, Lucy," he'd said, not meaning to be cruel, but sounding it just the same. "I have to learn to get on with things. We're only twenty-three. You can't spend the rest of your life pushing me around in a wheelchair, and I can't spend the rest of mine letting you!"

Despite all that had happened, he had achieved so much in such a short space of time, and she felt enormously proud of him. He could whizz about in his chair like a rocket now, had learned to drive a specially adapted car and

107

had even taken up wheelchair tennis.

"You never know," he'd told her. "I might even make the next Paralympics if I really work at it!"

He was starting to build a new and exciting life for himself, that was for sure, and she knew she had to show him that was OK, that she had come to terms with the way things were and was going to try to do the same. If only it was that easy!

Ahead of her, on the promenade, what looked like a whole army of squawking, scrabbling gulls had suddenly descended from the sky, flapping and dipping their huge white wings and jostling for space. They were fighting over the remains of someone's discarded bag of chips and making a terrible racket.

Beaks dipped furiously into the scrunched-up paper and grabbed what they could get, stopping only to peck at any other beak that came near enough to be a threat, not one of them ready to give up.

Their sheer determination intrigued her, and she couldn't help but admire them.

"That'll be Dan later today," she told herself as yet more birds swooped down out of the sky.

She checked her watch. Another three hours to wait, at least.

SHE could feel her heart pounding harder every time she thought about the parachute jump. OK, he would be strapped to an instructor. Tandem jumping, they called it. Everything would be checked and double-checked, made as safe as possible, but, even so, she was scared for him. Half of her wanted to be there to watch him do it, to cheer him on as he fell through the clouds, but the other half knew she wouldn't be able to.

The shock and pain of his accident had hit her almost as hard as it had him. They were twins, after all, as close as it was possible to be. If anything went wrong, if anything else terrible happened to him, she knew she wouldn't be able to bear it.

She almost wished that it would be as windy as this where he was, too, and that the whole jump idea would have to be abandoned. But that was just her own anguish talking, and she knew it wasn't fair of her to try to hold him back.

She picked up the small overnight bag at her feet, turned away from the force of the wind and, startling the gulls back into the air as she strode through their midst, made her way back towards the town.

She stopped at the first bed and breakfast place she came to with a *Vacancies* sign in the window. They all looked pretty much the same, and at this time of year finding somewhere with rooms available was never going to be hard.

"Just the one night, is it, love?" the landlady asked, handing over the key

Durham Cathedral

DURHAM Cathedral is a Norman building constructed between 1093 and 1133 in the Romanesque style. It is unique in architectural terms because it is the oldest surviving building with a stone-vaulted ceiling of such a large scale. Up until this point, most ceilings were made out of wood, but this building shaped the course of European architecture after its construction.

In fact, Durham World Heritage Site was inscribed by UNESCO in 1986 (among the first UK sites to be listed) in recognition of its Outstanding Universal Value. The site's architectural importance lies in the fact that Durham Cathedral and Castle are among the greatest monuments of the Norman Conquest of Britain, and Durham Cathedral is one of the finest examples of Norman architecture in Europe.

with a smile and pointing her towards the staircase.

Lucy nodded and bumped her bag up the stairs and along the short carpeted hallway until she found the small single room she had been allocated at the back of the house. There was no lift, but that didn't matter today, since she was on her own. If Dan had been here . . .

She pushed the thought aside and stood for a moment, taking in her surroundings: narrow bed with candlewick bedspread, wooden wardrobe and matching chest of drawers, and a wash basin with a single white towel hanging from a rail beside it. No bathroom (that, apparently, was shared and could be found at the end of the hall) or TV. No kettle for tea or coffee. But what had she expected? This wasn't a four-star hotel, just a cheap B&B by the sea, and no worse than some of the student rooms she and her friends had used at university.

Lucy parted the curtains and peered out over grey slate roofs and a small car park.

It might have been nice to have a view of the sea, but the house was too far back from the seafront, and the room was really only a base to leave her things in and return to later to sleep. Quickly changing into a warm shirt and jeans, and leaving everything else where she'd dropped it on the bed, she grabbed her handbag and coat and made her way back downstairs and outside into the chill of the afternoon.

There weren't many tourists about and all the main attractions were probably closed, but there would still be shelters and cafés, places to get out of the wind. Right now, there was nothing she needed more than a nice cup of strong tea and some time to think.

S HE found somewhere on the front: a small café, almost empty, but it looked warm and clean, so she chose a table by the window, hung her coat over the back of the chair, ordered tea and a bun, and settled down to watch the world go by.

She tried to remember where they had eaten the last time. These seaside eating places, like the bed and breakfast hotels, had a habit of all looking pretty much the same, with their checked cloths and big red sauce bottles, their catchy names and big steamy windows looking over the sea. They had probably eaten fish and chips, though. That had always been Dan's favourite.

She missed Dan whenever they were apart. Three years at university had done nothing to alter that, despite their joyous reunions at the end of every term and the constant e-mails and phone calls. And now he was off by himself again.

Not really alone, though, he had assured her. The rest of the guys from the rehab unit were there, too, all eager to push themselves to the limit and have some fun. All of them in the same boat.

She'd laughed when he'd said that.

"Plane, not boat!" she'd reminded him, but still she'd felt a silly pang of jealousy that he had other people to share his life and all his dreams with now.

Paul and Sean had become great friends, not only to Dan but to Lucy, too. Paul, married to his childhood sweetheart and who had only just become a father when he'd lost his right leg after being hit by a bus, and Sean, a police officer seriously injured in a high-speed chase. Three young men, embarking on a recovery programme together. All, as Dan had said, very much in the same boat, and closer to him than any of his old university friends, because they had all shared – and were still sharing – the same life-changing experience.

She didn't know how Dan would ever have coped without them.

And then there was Annie, of course. She had been a nurse on the ward when he'd first been in hospital but, as time had passed, she had gradually become much more than that.

Lucy was glad that Dan had found a girl who loved him and wanted to look after him, not because of his disability but in spite of it. And she would be there with the other three today, supporting them as they threw themselves out of that plane, just as she always did, no matter what they chose to do.

Lucy sometimes wished she could be more like Annie, just being with Dan as he was now and helping him to move on, instead of constantly making comparisons with the way things were before.

She took a sip of her tea and bit the cherry off the top of her bun, letting the heat of the tea and the sweetness of the cherry merge on her tongue. If she'd had a biscuit she would have dunked it, but the bun was too big to dip into the cup.

She smiled to herself, knowing what Dan would have done: pulled big chunks off and dunked them one at a time until the surface of the tea was bobbing with crumbs.

His body might have changed, but his character and his inner spirit were still there, just the same as ever, alive and kicking!

OUTSIDE the window, the gulls were back. Probably not the same ones, but just as tenacious and noisy as the group down by the sea earlier.

She watched them for a while, tearing busily at a thick crust of bread someone had thrown for them, not willing to give up on their find or even to move aside as two small boys on bikes rode straight past them, their speeding wheels just inches away.

A smaller bird waited at the back, standing away from the rest. One of its legs looked strangely misshapen, and it walked in an ungainly way, almost like an old man with a limp. Even from this distance, Lucy could tell that it had been injured in some way, or perhaps born with a deformity.

Either way, every time the bird made the effort to approach the others, one of them blocked its path and fought it back. She felt instantly sorry for it, left out of the action, hungry but unable to fight its way through the crowd.

She thought of Dan, and those first few months in the hospital, when all he had wanted was to be like everyone else, to merge into the crowd and walk again. How much she had wanted to reach out and protect him, to make all his pain go away.

But sometimes wishing just isn't enough, and they had both had to accept that, barring miracles, Dan would never walk again.

THE boys on bikes had doubled back, and were whooping and yelling to each other as they rattled past again, using the almost deserted pavement as a makeshift raceway.

She should have been annoyed, but at least it kept them out of the road and safe from all its dangers, something that Lucy had become intensely aware of these last two years.

The flock finally panicked and scattered, leaving just the little lame bird behind. Too badly injured to fly off with the others, she supposed, but at least now it had a clear run at the remains of the food.

And then her mobile phone rang.

"Lucy, I did it!" It was Dan's voice, sounding more excited and full of joy than he had in years.

Lucy dropped her bun on to its plate, her hand going straight to her mouth as the shock hit her.

"You've done it? Already? But you're not meant to be jumping until five o'clock!"

"Sorry, Luce. Little white lie. It was always scheduled for half-past three, weather conditions permitting. I just didn't want you to sit worrying. Then I'd have been worrying about you, and not concentrating on the jump. This way it's all over before you've had the chance to think about it.

"It was fantastic!" he went on. "Something I might never have had the courage to do before the crash. And I've made nearly four hundred pounds in sponsorship for charity. So that's twenty you owe me, remember?"

"I remember . . ."

"I've had the most brilliant day." He could hardly contain his excitement. "We all have. And it's not true what they say, you know: you don't have to learn to walk before you can run . . . or fly! My legs might have let me down, and a footballing career is definitely not a possibility, but I'm sure now that I'm going to try to make a real go of the tennis.

"I need something to aim for, Luce, and today's shown me that anything's possible. I can do this, with my friends around me, and a bit of moral support from you, of course . . ."

"I would have supported you today if you'd let me!" she protested.

Fifty Years Ago . . . **September 4, 1964**

THE Forth Road Bridge was officially opened by Her Majesty, Queen Elizabeth II, linking Fife and Edinburgh by road. The impressive bridge took six years to build, and sadly seven men lost their lives while working on it.

At a total length of 2,512 metres it was the longest suspension bridge span outside the United States and the fourth-longest span in the world at the time of its construction, and comprises 39,000 tonnes of steel and concrete.

Tollbooths collected the controversial tolls until early 2008 and, in spite of the costs, the bridge was crossed by some 2.5 million vehicles in its first year and carried its 250-millionth vehicle in 2002. It was closed for the first time in 2010 due to heavy snow.

It has become a famous landmark over the last 50 years and was conferred Listed Building Status by Historic Scotland in 2001.

"I know that. I just wanted to prove something to myself. Take a leap of faith, if you like. And I have. It was absolutely incredible. Annie filmed it all, too, so we can show you when we get back."

She noticed how easily he said that word "we". He and Annie were most definitely a couple now, but she didn't feel jealous at all any more. Dan was the happiest he had been in a long time, and Annie had helped bring that about.

Lucy was pleased for them.

In fact, she had to admit that she'd taken rather a fancy to his gorgeous dark-haired friend Sean, and she had a feeling he might feel the same way. It would be good for them all to spend time together, away from hospitals and rehab, just having fun for a change. Why should they let a couple of wheelchairs get in the way of that?

"But how about you?" Dan was saying. "What have you been doing with yourself while I've been away? Shopping, knowing you!"

"Yes, that's right." She wouldn't tell him she was here by the sea, reminiscing, moping into a teacup and feeling sorry for herself. Anyone would think it was her legs that had been crushed that day, rather than Dan's.

AND if he could pick himself up and be so brave about it, then so could she. Life had to go on, didn't it? Even if it was not quite the life you'd expected. Sometimes you just had to let go and take that leap of faith into the unknown.

"Yes, I'm out buying shoes again. You know me so well!"

She sent him a big "well-done" kiss down the line and rang off, grabbed her coat and walked back out on to the street, her legs wobbling just a little bit as she pushed away the picture that had come into her head, of her brother hurtling through the sky towards the ground.

She shrugged her arms back into her old comfy coat and sighed contentedly.

Shopping! Now, there was an idea. She was sure there was a shopping precinct around here somewhere. She remembered it from last time. And she really did need shoes, or new trainers at least, if she was going to be hanging around all those tennis courts.

She looked up, expecting to see signs of the rain that had been threatening ever since she'd arrived. But the sun was just starting to peep through a break in the clouds, and she had to raise her hand to shield her eyes from the unexpected brightness.

And then, with a whoosh past her ankles, the little seagull she had forgotten all about suddenly took off into the sky, a big piece of bread wedged in his beak, his damaged leg no longer obvious at all as he spread his big beautiful wings and flew off majestically towards the sun. ∎

My Little Sister

by Karen Byrom.

T HE single loose photograph had fallen out of the family album, one of several I'd carted home from my parents' house after Mum and Dad had decided to downsize to a small flat near the seaside. Not wanting to see family history consigned to the oversized skip Dad had hired, I'd volunteered my services as curator of the Carlin family memories, rashly promising to upload them all on to CDs.

That was three years ago. Instead, I'd come home, chucked them on top of a pile of my own photo albums – also waiting to be converted to digital – on the bottom shelf of my overflowing bookcase, and more or less forgotten about them. Until now.

But this evening my eight-year-old daughter, Lydie, had asked to look at my wedding album. While tugging it out I'd dislodged the older, dustier albums, and so the top one had given up its secret – a photograph from over 25 years ago.

Kneeling to retrieve it from where it had fallen, face down, I turned over the snap and found myself looking at a solemn-faced girl who gazed back at me with wide blue eyes, a very young baby in her lap.

It was an unusual photograph. Most little girls would probably be looking at the baby on their lap, smiling as Mum or Dad exhorted them to say "cheese" for the camera, hoping to capture a happy moment in time. But there was a sadness about this snap – a stillness that bespoke a lack of joy and even a sense of approaching crisis, too much for one small child to bear.

115

I was this girl in the photograph. And the baby was my precious little sister, Claire.

For years, I'd begged my parents to provide me with a little sister or brother – from the age of five, actually, when I went off to school and discovered that, of all the children in my class, I was the only "only"! All the other boys and girls had older brothers or sisters to tease and torment them, but ultimately to protect them. Or younger siblings they, in turn, could protect, tease and torment. Some lucky classmates had both. I felt a five-year-old's raw sense of injustice!

Looking back, my constant nagging must have hurt my parents quite badly. I don't remember all the various lighthearted excuses they gave, but I do remember the momentous day when I was eight and they sat me down and told me that, by Christmas, I'd have a new brother or sister.

To be honest, by then I wasn't too bothered. I'd made lots of friends at school and had learned with them to regard younger siblings as a bit of a nuisance. But I was a sensitive child – the fruit of too much time spent in adult company – and so I smiled and hugged them both and assured them that I wouldn't be jealous.

And I wasn't. I was secure in their love, and happy enough about the coming baby.

"Gemma's such an easy child," I remember Gran saying when she thought I wasn't in earshot.

"Let's hope this one is," Mum replied. "It certainly isn't giving me an easy time just now."

How could that be when it wasn't even born yet, I wondered before I wandered off, indifferent, on my own ploys. I was aware the coming baby was making my mum sick and a bit tired, but, looking back, I now know she and Dad went to great lengths to conceal just how poorly she was.

CHRISTMAS was still two months away when I awoke one morning and wandered down to the kitchen to find Gran there instead of Mum, bustling about with cereal bowls and milk.

"Where are Mum and Dad?" I asked, eyeing her suspiciously. I loved my gran, but her presence at breakfast was definitely out of the ordinary.

"They've had to go out," Gran said shortly. "Now, sit down and eat your cereal, Gemma, then get ready for school, there's a good girl."

"Out where?" I demanded, holding on to the back of my chair.

Gran sighed, then must have reluctantly decided I would be satisfied with nothing but the truth.

"To the hospital," she said. "The baby's decided to come a little early. It's not here yet," she went on, forestalling my next question. "Your dad will phone soon enough."

I pondered that as I sat down, obedient for now, and spooned up my breakfast. So it had decided to come early. Did this baby have a mind of its own, then? I thought babies lay around, just . . . being, until they were old enough to walk and talk! For the first time I began to feel more than a mild interest in my new baby brother or sister.

But Gran's unease had communicated itself to me, and I went off to school feeling dissatisfied, hoping Dad would be home by the time I came back, even if Mum had to stay in hospital with the baby.

He wasn't. It was still Gran, and I could tell she had been crying, although she put on a brave smile as she told me I now had a little sister.

"Mum and Dad are staying with her for now," she said. "So it's just me and you for tonight."

"Can we go and see her?"

Gran bit her lip.

"Not yet, Gemma. She's too little. She's been born a bit early, remember. They wouldn't let you in to see her yet."

"Not fair!" I pouted. Then, "What's for tea, Gran? Can we have ice-cream for afters?"

"Anything at all, Gemma," Gran agreed readily.

That, if nothing else, should have told me something was wrong.

IT was six days before I saw baby Claire. Dad came home the next day. He couldn't keep the tremor from his voice as he sat me down and explained in words that I would understand that the baby was very poorly. Dimly I grasped that she might not come home at all, and for the first time, the enormity of events hit me.

I was allowed to see Mum, of course. She smiled so bravely and cheerfully for me that somehow I never doubted that all would be well. As the weeks went by, Dad began to look happier, too. Two days after Mum came home – without the baby – he went back to work.

"Say hello to Claire for me," he said, dropping a kiss on my head on his way out of the door. For the momentous day had come at last. Mum was taking me to see the baby!

I'd been warned so much about Claire's tininess, and the "poorly heart" that was keeping her in hospital, that I was almost afraid to approach the crib in the baby's intensive care unit. All around me, scary-looking machines hummed and lights flashed. Nurses glided between the cots, murmuring low so as not to startle the fragile babies in their care. In the distance, a woman was crying.

But all paled into stillness as I looked down at my little sister. I hardly saw the wires that covered her body, or the tube poking out from her poor little nose. I just saw the bright blue eyes, so like mine, fix on me as she sensed my presence above her.

Without any urging I put my hand through the vent that allowed me to make contact with her. As I took hold of her hand I felt her little fingers curl around mine.

And my eight-year-old heart dissolved. Now I knew what being a big sister involved.

Right there and then, I vowed to myself to protect her for ever.

"She'll be home soon." The nurse hovering at the top of the crib smiled at me. "Then you'll be able to hold her properly."

"Really?" I turned to Mum. It didn't seem possible that this little bundle could survive without all the tubes and wires.

Mum pressed my spare hand.

"She's a lot bigger and stronger now. She will still need an operation when she's a little older. But, yes, she'll be home soon."

*　*　*　*

Claire did come home, and I doted on her, clamouring to be the one to hold her, feed and change her. I'd have slept by her side if they'd let me, but Mum and Dad insisted I stay in my own room at night.

"You need your sleep if you're going to shine at school and set a good example to your little sister."

So to school I went, to boast about the baby and how much she looked like me, and how she smiled for me and no-one else, till my chums lost interest and left.

But they left me with my happy daydreams where I was teaching Claire to walk and to talk and to climb trees and read storybooks, and join me in bugging Mum and Dad about getting a puppy, or at least a kitten to take care of.

BEFORE that, however, there was the operation to face.
Eight weeks after she came home from hospital, the day before my ninth birthday, I had to say goodbye to Claire as Mum packed a bag for herself and the baby. Dad was driving them to Great Ormond Street, hundreds of miles away.

I was staying at home with Gran.

"Why can't I go, too?" I moaned, already knowing the answer. We'd been through this many times.

Gran hugged me tightly as, white-faced, Mum continued her packing.

Dad looked round at us all.

"Come on, girls!" he said in an attempt to be cheery. "I'll be back in a couple of days, and Mum and Claire will be home before you know it." He disappeared into the dining-room and reappeared, waving his camera. "Let's have an early birthday snap, Gemma, in case Gran can't figure out how to use the camera tomorrow."

"Yes," Mum echoed. "One more picture for the album."

Gently, she took Claire from her carrycot and settled her carefully in my arms.

"Say cheese!" Dad said. But I couldn't smile for him. My little sister, so warm, so precious, so content, was going so far away from me. And I was old enough now to know that my elders were just putting on a brave front for my benefit.

Dad took the photograph. Gently, I bent and kissed Claire, then delivered her up to my mother. Before my parents were in the car I was up in my room, ignoring Gran's calls, sobbing into my pillow as if my heart would break, wondering when, if ever, I would see my little sister again.

THE sound of the doorbell roused me from my reverie, and I got to my feet, laying the photograph to one side.

But someone reached the door before me.

"Auntie Claire! Auntie Claire!" I heard Lydie's piercing squeals as my sister floated into the hall in a cloud of fragrance and romance. Her eyes, still as blue as mine, were bright and happy as she scooped Lydie up into her arms.

"How's my littlest bridesmaid?" she asked Lydie, waltzing her around the room.

Forgetting her eight-year-old dignity, Lydie laughed with joy as, breathless, they both sank on to the bottom step of the stairs.

"She's supposed to be getting ready for bed," I replied, raising my left eyebrow at them both. "Don't get her too excited now, Claire, or she won't be fit for tomorrow. Maybe we should give that dress to Ellie, next door?" I teased.

Like a shot, Lydie was out of the room.

"I'm going! I'm going!" she called from halfway up the stairs. "But, Mum, can we please look at your wedding photos before I go to sleep? You promised ages ago!"

"She's gone wedding daft!" I smiled, gathering my little sister in for a hug. "How about you? All set for the big day?"

"As set as I'll ever be." Claire grinned. "Especially with you by my side as my matron of honour, Gemma."

In a sudden rush of emotion, I took her hand.

"Always, Claire."

Yes, her soon-to-be husband, Matthew, would love and cherish her, but there's nothing like a big sister when you need one. From the day she'd come home from Great Ormond Street, a pinker, healthier baby than any of us had dared to hope, I'd been by her side.

As her big sister it was my job to tease and torment and, above all, protect her. And as she responded to the squeeze of my hand, I knew Claire knew I would always be there for her. ■

Stage Fright

by David Pickering.

BLUE heaven, and you and I.
And sand kissing a moonlit sky."
I sang the words to myself as I walked down the lane to the village hall, on a warm late-August evening in 1970.

It seemed a shame to be thinking of winter pastimes, but I'd been looking forward to this evening since last April, when the curtain came down on the Cranberry Hill Amateur Operatic Society's final performance of "The Merry Widow".

My best friend, Penny, had been superb as Anna, the scheming widow, and Penny's husband, Matt, had made every female heart flutter with his portrayal of the dashing Count Danilo.

At the after-show party, our chairman, Bill Gordon, thanked all those members who had helped to make the show a huge success.

Even I got a mention.

"Jane, our indispensable tea lady," was Bill's description of me.

He made a farewell presentation to Mr Parker, our departing musical director, thanking him for many years of service, and then continued.

"And now for the name of next year's show."

The crowded room buzzed with excitement.

"Our audiences love the old-fashioned shows," Bill said. "And so, the committee has chosen 'The Desert Song'."

I gasped with delight. It was my favourite show. It had such gorgeous music and lovely parts for the lucky chosen few.

I knew that Penny would jump at the chance to play Margot, the mischievous, romance-seeking heroine. I certainly would, I thought, if only I was good enough.

Now, as I tiptoed across the foyer of the village hall, I could already hear music from the forthcoming show being expertly played on the piano. I crept in through the inner door. A dark-haired stranger was sitting at the keyboard, his fingers dancing over the keys.

He looked up and smiled.

"Good evening."

"Er, hello. I'm sorry to barge in," I said. "I just need to get to the . . ." I waved an arm in the direction of the kitchen, and made a dash for it.

I'd just filled the boiler and switched it on when the first strains of "Blue Heaven" wafted through from the hall.

I paused to listen. Then I began to sing.

"A desert breeze whisp'ring a lullaby,

Illustration by Mike Heslop.

Only stars above you to see I love you."

As the music swelled, a thrill ran down my spine.

"Oh, give me that night divine,

And let my arms in yours entwine,

The desert song . . ."

The melody spluttered and died on my lips as the tall, smiling figure of the stranger appeared in the open doorway. I'd been so swept away that I hadn't realised the piano had stopped, and I was singing at the top of my voice.

"S-sorry," I stammered. "Was I disturbing you?"

"Not a bit. I just came to find out who was joining in so enthusiastically." His eyes crinkled into a gentle smile. "Will you be auditioning for a part this evening?"

"Me? Good heavens, no."

"Have you ever played a part?"

"Only once."

"Really?" He sounded surprised, although I couldn't think why. "Do you sing in the chorus, then?"

"Not since Mother was taken ill," I replied. "This was her job, you see. I took over to help out."

"Well, I hope your mother will soon be well again."

I glanced up at him.

"Mother died last year."

"Oh, I am sorry." He came closer. "How clumsy of me. Do, please, forgive me."

I looked up into his deep-blue eyes and, for several moments, neither of us spoke. I swallowed hard and looked away.

"I can't offer you a cup of tea yet. The boiler won't be ready for another twenty minutes."

"Not to worry. People will be arriving soon, I expect. I'm Rick Markham, the new musical director."

I shook the large, strong hand that he held out and, once again, I found myself gazing into those deep and extraordinarily intense blue eyes.

A burst of laughter came from the hall.

"It sounds as if we've got company already." He smiled again and released my hand. "I'd better go."

FOR the next three hours the rafters rang with the sound of hopeful members of the society going through their auditions.

Their ordeal done, each of them came into the kitchen for a much-needed cup of tea and a comforting buttered scone or a slice of fruitcake.

As I scooted around, tending to everyone's needs, my mind kept wandering back to the time when I first considered joining the society – 12 years ago.

I'd just left school and I thought I was grown-up. I wanted to play romantic leads and wear beautiful costumes. In reality, I was sixteen and painfully shy, with unflattering NHS glasses perched on my nose.

I remember sitting on my bed, fiddling with my hair, while Mother, lovingly but firmly, laid down the law.

"Jane, you have to get out there and join in; show people what you can do. At least have a go!"

Two days later, and still scared stiff, I auditioned for "The Sound Of Music". I didn't expect anything; a place in the chorus, a nun, perhaps.

Mr Parker gave me a friendly smile.

"That was very nice, Jane. Would you like to play Liesl?"

The eldest of the von Trapp children! Would I? I raced all the way home and arrived so out of breath I could scarcely blurt out the news.

Mother was just as excited. To give me some support, she joined the society, too. She'd been lonely since Dad died and she enjoyed making new friends and helping with refreshments.

I met Matt at my first rehearsal. He was playing Rolf the post-boy, my onstage love-interest.

For a seventeen-year-old, he had a surprisingly mellow, light baritone voice, and his smile dazzled all the ladies; especially me. Rehearsals were an absolute joy.

One evening I asked Mother if I could invite him home for supper, and it became a regular occurrence.

We chattered non-stop.

"I'd love to play Eliza Doolittle in 'My Fair Lady'," I'd say. "And Margot in 'The Desert Song'."

"I'm sure you will, one day, my love," Mother would chip in. "Meanwhile, pass Matt the cheese and biscuits, will you?"

Sadly, the excitement didn't survive my first show. Lacking Matt's self-confidence, and struggling without my glasses, I found the stage a big, scary place.

One night, I bumped into the scenery, rebounded and trod on the leading lady's corns.

"Doh, a deer," she sang. "A female a-a-a-agh!" Safe to say, I was never again one of her favourite things.

AFTERWARDS I sobbed on Matt's shoulder, while he tried valiantly to console me.

"That was an accident," he said. "It could have happened to anyone. Your time will come."

Not everyone agreed. For the next show I was banished to the back row of the chorus, and there I stayed. Matt, meanwhile, went on to play bigger and bigger parts.

We'd been members for about five years when Penny joined the society. I
liked her from the start, bubbly and friendly as she was, with sparkling eyes and
a glorious voice.

It soon became obvious that she and Matt were made for each other, onstage
and off, and no-one was surprised when their make-believe romances began to
blossom into the real thing.

"Jane . . ." Matt started hesitantly one evening ". . . you're not upset about
Penny and me, are you? I mean, it's not as if there's ever been anything, well . . .
serious, between you and me."

He was right, of course, there never had been – although I'd often wondered
if one day, perhaps . . .

"We've just been friends," he went on. "Dear friends! And we still can be."

"Of course we'll still be friends," I said. "I want that just as much as you
do."

Eighteen months later, I was Penny's chief bridesmaid, and the three of us
have always stayed very close.

When Mother was taken ill, Penny sat for endless hours keeping me
company, often through long, weary nights. Matt did all my running about,
collecting prescriptions and doing my shopping.

They were there the night that Mother slipped peacefully away, and they
were a tower of strength and comfort in the tearful weeks that followed.

When I returned to the society, I couldn't face going back onstage, not even
in the chorus.

"You could, perhaps, take over your mother's old job," Bill Gordon
suggested.

I agreed. It would be one way of being useful.

Suddenly, my reminiscences were interrupted as, once again, "Blue Heaven"
floated through from the hall, this time sung by Matt's unmistakeable baritone,
deeper now, rich and mature.

ALONE in the kitchen, I closed my eyes. Yes, I could just imagine him
as the mysterious outlaw, the masked Red Shadow.
"Hey!" A bright voice made me jump. "No sleeping on the job!" I
opened my eyes to see Penny grinning at me from the doorway.

"Matt sounds in good voice," I said. "Are you raring to go?"

"No. I'm not taking part in this show."

My chin dropped.

"What? Why on earth not?"

"Well, by next spring I shall be in no fit shape."

"Why? Are you ill?"

A delighted smile lit Penny's pretty face.

"No. I'm fine." She laughed gleefully. "Jane, I'm having a baby."

"Oh, Penny!" I wrapped her in a great, joyful hug, and tears filled my eyes.

"That's wonderful. I'm so, so happy for you!" Then another thought struck me. "But who's going to play Margot?"

Penny shrugged.

"Not me."

"Do the committee know?"

"We're going to tell them when Matt's finished. We wanted you, as godmother, to be the first to know."

"Godmother? Oh!" And now the tears spilled over and flooded down my cheeks.

HALF an hour later, I was still sniffling as I tidied up the kitchen. The hall was silent except for the muffled hum of committee voices, deep in deliberation. The kitchen door opened, and I turned to see Bill Gordon eyeing me uncertainly.

"Oh, Bill. Do you want some more tea? I've turned the boiler off and put everything away."

"It's not that, Jane. Could you come through? We'd like a word with you."

I followed Bill into the hall. The members of the committee sat along the length of a trestle table. Only Rick's smile lit up an otherwise gloomy assembly.

"Jane," he began. "We're having trouble casting the part of Margot. We have options, but Penny and Matt suggested someone else we should consider." He paused. "They suggested you."

"Me?"

"They said that, after all these years, it's high time the society gave you another chance. After that little burst in the kitchen, I'd love to hear you sing again. Will you audition for us?"

I felt the colour drain from my cheeks.

"I'd rather not. I mean . . . I can't! Really, I can't!"

"I've got the music here, if you need it."

"No, I know the music . . . and all the words."

"Well, then, at least have a go. Show us what you can do!"

I didn't respond. I simply stood there, my mind in a whirl. I was thinking about Mother's words, all those years ago; words which Rick had just echoed.

I also thought about Penny and Matt. They'd be back home by now, but I knew they were willing me on, urging me to take my chance.

Then I realised that Rick was watching me intently and, as our eyes met, I knew that he wanted me to succeed. I also knew that I wanted to – for his sake as well as my own, and for all those who'd ever loved and encouraged me.

Rick broke the silence.

"Will you try, Jane?"

I bit my lip and hesitated. Then I nodded.

For the next 20 minutes or so, something quite astonishing happened; something mysterious and beautiful. With Rick's gentle encouragement, all my shyness evaporated, and with it went every one of my inhibitions.

I sang, I danced, I acted. I poured out my heart and soul. I didn't just play Margot – I *was* Margot; fun-loving, romantic and passionate.

As the final notes echoed around the hall, Rick turned to the committee.

"Ladies and gentlemen, I think –"

I didn't hear any more. I was suddenly very cold, and the room was spinning. A million miles away, Rick began to shout. Chair legs scraped. Feet clattered. Then I felt strong arms around me, supporting me and lifting me on to a chair.

My knees were still shaking when Rick drew to a halt at my gate after driving me home.

"Why me?" I asked.

"Because you have a beautiful voice, and the way you performed those numbers was simply breathtaking."

"But I couldn't even get through the audition without fainting. What if I'm a complete disaster?"

Rick smiled.

"You'll be wonderful. You have talent, and I'll give you all the help I can."

"You must have better things to do than worry about me," I said.

"I shall have a school concert to conduct, just before Christmas, but apart from that, all my evenings are yours."

"Are you a teacher?"

"Yes. I teach music at High Field Secondary. I can't wait for the new term to start. I just love opening young minds to the joy of music."

I realised that I was staring hard at my companion, lost in his words, entranced by his gentle smile.

I shook myself.

"Look," I said. "Why don't you come in for a cup of tea?"

"Thank you, but I must go home and get a meal. I came here straight from school. I haven't eaten since breakfast."

"Then you must come in and let me cook something for you. It's the least I can do. I won't take no for an answer!"

A LITTLE before midnight, I stood at the gate, watching Rick drive away. The darkness was soft and warm, and the night felt strangely enchanted.

"Well, Mum," I murmured. "Has my time come at last? Leading lady! And that's not all. My life might be changing in other ways as well."

Rick slowed down at the bend in the lane and waved through the open car window. As I waved back, "Blue Heaven" crept again into my head. Softly, I sang the closing lines.

"The desert song calling
Its voice enthralling,
Will make you mine . . ." ■

I MARCHED up the drive, turned the key in the lock more forcefully than was strictly necessary and pushed my front door open.

I stomped through to the kitchen, deposited my handbag on the table and put the kettle on. I was expecting my oldest and best friend, Nancy, to tea and had only just got back in time.

by Nina Waglé.

I sighed. My feet were aching from having spent the past three hours in a pointless trawl of the shops and I was reminded that I was no longer as young as I used to be. Though, to be truthful, the aching feet had nothing to do with my age (sixty-five), and everything to do with my shoes.

I do love shoes and am sometimes guilty of choosing style over sense. With hindsight, my high-heeled purple shoes had not been the best of choices, even if they did have a jaunty little bow attached to the side.

The trouble was that I hadn't planned on spending three hours shopping. And I hadn't planned on the whole trip being for nothing. I had underestimated how hard it would be to find a suitable significant birthday present for my granddaughter. Because, you see, it needed to be significant.

Partly because Gwen would be twenty-five, a significant age, and partly because Gwen was about to set

Illustration by Gerard Fay.

It's The Thought That Counts

up a business of her own – a café in the high street.

But mostly, of course, because I love her. Gwen and I have always been close – she was my first grandchild and we seemed to have a special bond from the moment I laid eyes on her. Plus, I have been lucky to have had a very hands-on role in her life.

My daughter, Libby, went back to work two days a week when Gwen was one and asked if I would look after Gwen. Of course I was more than happy to help out and look after my beautiful granddaughter. In some ways, I think Libby hoped it would be therapeutic for me, as my beloved husband, Archie, had sadly passed away just before Gwen was born.

I like to think that Gwen got her first inspiration for her café from those early days with me. Like my mother before me, and her mother before her, I had been brought up with a love of baking and cooking.

The cooking gene had completely missed Libby, so it was lovely for me to see the enjoyment Gwen got from preparing food. We spent hours playing café, using a second-hand toy oven that I found in a jumble sale, along with lots of extremely real-looking plastic fruit.

From plastic food and a wooden oven we graduated on to the real thing and spent many happy hours in the kitchen. And now here was Gwen all ready to set up her very own café and catering business.

I heard the ring of the front doorbell and went to let Nancy in.

She took one look at me and, barely waiting to sit down, she asked, "Rosie, what's wrong?"

I sighed.

"I can't find Gwen a present," I said.

"How about a book? Or a voucher? Or some clothes?"

"Not significant enough," I said and launched into my explanation.

Nancy eyed me with the knowledge of 50 years of friendship.

"There's something else as well, isn't there?" she said. "Another reason why this present is so important to you."

"It's just . . ." I crumbled a chocolate digestive between my fingers. "It's just Harry," I blurted out.

NANCY looked puzzled. As well she might. Harry is Gwen's grandfather from her dad's side.

"What's Harry got to do with it?" Nancy asked.

I stared down into my cup of tea.

"He's buying her an oven."

Nancy looked even more puzzled, and just a mite confused.

"And that's a problem because . . .?" she asked.

"It's not a problem," I said a shade defensively. "It's just that I want to give her something equally meaningful."

"It's not a competition, Rosie," my best friend said sternly. And quite

Dunrobin Castle

TRADITIONALLY, British castles are utilitarian constructions – solid, chunky buildings designed to withstand the rigours of warfare throughout the ages. Although Dunrobin Castle still has the original fortified keep at its heart, it has grown into something more like a French chateau, with high spires and magnificent turrets overlooking its picturesque gardens.

Roughly an hour's drive north of Inverness, this is the most northerly of Scotland's great houses, and contains 189 rooms. It's been the home of the Earls and Dukes of Sutherland since the 13th century, and was extensively remodelled into its current Baronial style in the middle of the 19th century. The castle and gardens are open to the public.

rightly, I might add. She certainly wasn't saying anything I hadn't thought myself.

"I do know that," I said. "I am truly happy that Gwen is getting the oven. And I can see that it is really generous of Harry. I just want to feel that I am giving her something significant, too. I want her to see how proud I am of her."

"Oh, Rosie," Nancy said. "Gwen knows that. You've been there for her every step of the way. Why don't you make her some tablecloths? For the café. You know how good you are at making things."

I pictured the scene. A few tablecloths (that I had promised to make for Gwen anyway) versus a state-of-the-art oven.

Because this oven wasn't any old oven. This was the oven of Gwen's dreams. When she had told us all about it at a family Sunday dinner the previous week, I had seen the stars in her eyes. Somehow I didn't think red-checked tablecloths had star-making qualities.

I sighed.

"I'll think of something," I said.

"Why don't you talk to Harry about it?" Nancy suggested. "Maybe he will have a great idea. Maybe there's something that goes with the oven."

I looked at her.

"I probably can't even afford the handle of the oven," I pointed out. "And, anyway, I don't seem to be very good at talking to Harry," I added.

That was certainly true. I mean, until two months ago, when he moved up here from London, I'd never had much opportunity to speak to Harry. Of course, I met him and his wife, Margaret, at Libby and Steve's wedding, and then at various christenings, but even at those events I had spent more time talking to Margaret than to him.

SADLY, Margaret passed away two years ago, and then two months ago, Harry retired from his job as a business advisor in the banking world and relocated up here.

To be honest, I still hadn't talked to him much. I tried, really I did, but if I'm honest I've always found Harry rather intimidating. He wears pin-striped suits, ties and crisp white shirts, almost as though he hasn't realised retirement has caught up with him.

I was always worried he would expect me to be able to converse about prestigious banking jobs in the city, or that he was politely looking down on me because I'd never had a real career.

I did some part-time reception work when the children were at school, and I currently worked as a volunteer in a charity shop two mornings a week, but I couldn't help thinking that that was pretty small potatoes compared to mergers, acquisitions and whatever else Libby had mentioned Harry being involved with over the years.

So, somehow, whenever I saw him I became very flustered and started talking and talking – words just poured from my mouth in a stream of pure gibberish. The man probably thought I was verging on insane.

So you can imagine my surprise when, the following morning, I opened the door and there was Harry on the doorstep, immaculate in smart dark-grey trousers, crisp white shirt and paisley tie.

My surprise must have shown on my face.

He hesitated.

"I should have called first, but . . ."

I didn't let him finish, convinced that he thought I wasn't the sort of person you could just drop in on. Madly overcompensating, I started to usher Harry into the house like some sort of insane cattle herder, burbling about tea and coffee and wondering whether or not I had any of the posh biscuits left.

I COULD hardly blame him for the look of alarm on his face, or for grabbing the jar of instant coffee that I was waving at him, or for bellowing, "Rosie! It's OK. Instant is fine. And any biscuit will do me. I just want to talk."

I opened my mouth, ready to launch into a wordy agreement, when he shook his head.

"I want to talk," he said. "Please."

It was only then that I realised, in all our recent meetings, I really had never let the poor man say anything. I'd been so busy imagining what he was thinking that I'd never actually listened to him.

I sat down.

"I want to talk to you about the oven," he went on.

"It's a very generous present and Gwen is thrilled," I said, knowing the words, though sincere, sounded stilted. I was about to keep talking, to try to sound more gracious, and then remembered I was supposed to be listening.

Harry fidgeted, moving the jar of coffee to and fro across the table.

"I didn't expect Gwen to announce it like that," he said. "And I can see it may have made you feel a bit upset." He sighed. "I didn't want you to think I was showing off." He fidgeted with his tie. "And I just wanted to say sorry if I've been a bit stand-offish."

I pressed my lips together, holding words back.

"I suppose I have been a bit envious of your relationship with her," he blurted out finally.

I raised my eyebrows in mute question.

"Living so far away meant we never really saw the grandchildren enough. Don't get me wrong, Steve and Libby were very good at bringing the kids to see us, but it's not the same as being round the corner."

I gave up. I had to speak.

"Gwen has really appreciated having you around recently, though," I said.

"Your business knowledge has been invaluable." I had meant to sound encouraging, but I just sounded glum, with a smidgeon of bitter mixed in.

"Not as invaluable as you, teaching her how to cook using the recipes of generations ago," he said.

I glanced up in surprise. His tone was one of gloom, laced with a soupçon of vinegar.

Could it be that Harry was actually feeling the same as I was? That it was hard for him to come along and see how close Gwen and I were because it made him feel he had missed out? Just like it was hard for me to have another grandparent come along and steal my thunder?

We stared at each other for a long moment and suddenly the humour of the situation hit us both and we began to laugh.

Well, there is nothing like a really good laugh to clear the air. When we had finally stopped I stood up to put the kettle on.

"How about we start again?" I suggested, bringing out the chocolate digestives.

So we did, and an hour later I felt like a fool.

I'd been so busy being intimidated by a suit and my own envy that I hadn't seen what really counted. This man loved his granddaughter just as much as I did. He wasn't stand-offish, and when I explained to him the problems I was having choosing Gwen a present, he pondered for a few minutes and then beamed at me.

"I have an idea," he said.

"You do?" I asked.

He did.

O N Gwen's birthday, we all went to have a look at her brand-new premises and we admired the oven.

Then I stepped forward and handed Gwen a book. A book that I had put together myself. I had bound it carefully, using my scrapbooking skills, and I was pretty proud of the end result.

"It's a recipe book," I explained. "All the recipes that have been handed down from generation to generation. I thought you could cook traditional recipes in your brand-new state-of-the-art oven," I said.

"And," I continued, "Harry and I were wondering if you would like a couple of volunteers to help you out in the café."

Gwen positively beamed at both of us before hugging us.

"That is a marvellous idea," she said.

I turned to Harry.

"In that case, I guess a shopping trip is in order," I said.

I'd already spotted the perfect pair of shoes. They combined style and sense (shocking pink flat pumps with gorgeous red bows). As for Harry, I had my eye on a jazzy bow-tie that I knew would look very debonair on him. ∎

The Kindness Of Strangers

by Alison Carter.

THE announcements on the station loudspeakers didn't make any sense to me. They were a wash of harsh, echoing sound and I couldn't make out two words in a row.

"Platform fourteen." I heard that much, but was that the train to Eastbourne or to Brighton? If it was my train, how long did I have before it would leave?

Before getting on any train, I needed flowers. It was very important that I bought flowers before I got on that train. The flower stall in the centre of the concourse was enormous, or so it seemed to me that day. A very young girl swayed, listening to music from one ear on a pair of fluffy headphones as I stood, trying to choose. She seemed more interested in her music than potential customers.

133

The bouquets and buckets were piled up to my shoulder level – every colour, every type of flower. There were almost too many. Images crowded into my head of all those foreign lands where the flowers had been grown, and all the chattering pickers and the carts, the ships and lorries that had brought them here.

This wasn't like me at all. I had got myself into a right state. It was my sister's fault. She had gone into hospital very suddenly. It had been quite a shock.

I hadn't been the same since I picked up the phone at work and my dad spoke to me, solemnly and seriously. It wasn't like my dad to phone me at work, so I knew right away that something was wrong.

Fifteen minutes later, I'd called Mike to make sure he'd be home for the kids, I'd told my team to carry on without me, and I was on the slowest tube ever to Victoria station.

Now, I had to get flowers for Vicky and my brain had gone to mush.

"Can I help ya?" The girl with the headphones used a tone of voice which suggested she wasn't particularly keen to help, and I shook my head and stared at the carnations.

Vicky does not like carnations. That was the only fact I could fix on. No-one would believe that I head a 12-strong team in a large charity in central London. I am efficient and purposeful – usually. But when your sister has collapsed with something nobody can yet identify, even the strongest person would find it hard to cope.

I just knew that I had to take flowers. Of course, looking back now I can see that the flowers were the least important thing that day. I simply had to get there and be there for Vicky. But I always take my sister flowers. It's been a tradition for many years, a bond my sister and I share.

IT'S been that way since I was in trouble at university, heartbroken over some worthless boy. I was thinking I'd never love again and that it was the end of life as I knew it – you know the sort of thing. Vicky had hopped on a train and travelled from one end of the country to the other to help me out of my dark hole.

"I got you flowers," she said as I opened the door to my grotty bed-sit, tearstained and bleary-eyed.

We'd never bought each other flowers before. We'd never even bothered with proper birthday presents. We knew we loved each other, that we would do anything to help the other, but we didn't really go in for formal gift exchanging. Up until then, I'd bought her lipstick if I thought it would suit her and she'd bought me earrings because she knew they would go with my new top.

"They're dead," I said.

Vicky looked down at the bunch of tulips, wrapped in a plastic bag, that

134

she was carrying. They drooped badly.

"Oh, yeah," she said thoughtfully. "Maybe I should have bought them at this end rather than at Edinburgh Waverley five hours ago."

I began to laugh and she handed me the drooping flowers, which made me laugh more, and then she pushed past me into the room.

"Oh, shut up, you ungrateful wretch," she said. "Where do you keep the kettle in this hole and is it safe to drink from?"

Those dead tulips began my recovery. And ever since, every time either of us was in trouble, wherever we were, we'd bring flowers. We didn't always stick to conventional bunches of flowers, though. Once I got her a weird fly-eating item in a pot, from a posh shop near my office.

Vicky had been let go from a science lab assistant job she loved. I drove to Cardiff with that pot. It smelled bizarre the whole way down in the car. She took pictures on her phone of the thing eating flies, and e-mailed them to me. By doing that she told me that she was OK again and I could relax.

So, you can see why I had to have flowers for my sister. I could tell she was properly ill from the scared sound of Dad's voice. But there was all this choice. What was I going to do?

I screwed up my eyes and scanned the departures board. The six minutes past one – that was my train. It was now three minutes to. I had nine minutes to get flowers. That should be enough time, shouldn't it? I often did practically a week's shop in the supermarket near Victoria between a late-running meeting ending at half-past five and my five-to-six train home. Easy.

But today I was shaking and my faculties seemed impaired. What was wrong with me and what was I going to get? Tulips took me back to the bed-sit and somehow that was all wrong. Vicky hates carnations. I couldn't get beyond that. I was a grown woman of forty, dithering pathetically in front of a flower stall.

Some nice big purple flowers caught my eye. I couldn't remember their name, though, and my frantic brain told me I couldn't buy flowers that I couldn't name. There was a big bucket of gypsophilla and greenery, so I could get the girl to arrange some of that around the lilies. There were lots of lilies. But weren't lilies gloomy? I only had nine minutes and I could not remember. Eight minutes now.

What about roses? The only problem was that they looked a little tired and I wanted these flowers to be right.

WHEN Vicky woke up I had to be right there, holding beautiful flowers that would make her smile. Freesias? Didn't they have a strong smell? Maybe she'd feel poorly, or maybe the person in the next bed would object.

Irises? No, I'd taken irises last time, for her and Jonah's anniversary. These flowers had to say how much I cared. You might be forgiven for saying that flowers were a materialistic way to communicate – they cost quite a lot of money, after all – but they were our way.

There was a huge tub of chrysanthemums, bright yellow and white, and I had almost settled on those when my head began to swim and I started to perspire. I dropped my handbag between my feet and just stood there like a block of ice as thousands of people surged around me.

Most of them ignored me. One man in a long coat pushed me as he passed, and tutted. A porter swerved his baggage trolley to avoid me. I was frozen by this one tiny decision.

And then a young woman's face appeared in front of me.

"Let me get that for you. You don't want to leave your handbag down in here – it'll disappear in a second!" She handed me my handbag and looked at me with a questioning expression.

"You all right?" I heard her say in a strong London accent, speaking to a smiling toddler in a buggy.

"Too many of them, ain't there?" she said, waving a skinny hand at the banks of blooms.

It was as though she could read my mind.

"Yes, there are," I said.

"What d'you need them for?" She handed the toddler a carton of juice and deftly popped the straw in for him.

I stared at her, and I suppose the desperation in my face told her something. She was a little thing, no more than twenty, her hair scraped back, dressed in a sparkly hoodie and tight leggings.

"Visiting someone?" she asked, as though she was picking through my confused, lost brain.

I concentrated.

"The hospital," I said, "in . . ."

I had forgotten the name.

"Never mind. What does the person you're visiting like?"

I pointed to the carnations.

"She doesn't like those."

The girl laughed.

"Well, that rules out one per cent of the available stock! I'm Jasmine, by the way."

We stood there, me in my nice Jaeger suit and my briefcase, a complete mess, and her in six-inch heels and thick eyeliner, sorting it all out. She didn't look like a guardian angel, but she definitely was one.

SHE began to talk about flowers, and told me what she liked. She asked when my train was due to leave and I told her.

"Oh, we're on that one, my little lad and me. Going down to see my mum and dad," she said cheerfully.

136

Fifty Years Ago . . .
October 10, 1964

THE Games of the XVIII Olympiad, better known as the 1964 Summer Games, took place in Tokyo, later than usual in October. A series of firsts is noted for these games – they were the first to take place in an Asian country, they were the first games from which South Africa was banned and they were the first to be broadcast internationally via satellite. Previous Olympic games had been filmed and the tapes flown overseas to news stations.

British runner Ann Packer set a world record in the 800m, having never run the distance at international level prior to the Games. She ran on a cinder track – the last time this surface was used for the Games.

The British team returned home with a medal tally of four Golds, 12 Silver and two Bronze to finish 10th in the medal table.

I was calming down now and could feel the world coming back into focus. I saw her glance at the station display board.

"We've still got five minutes," she said.

"No problem."

The toddler began to grizzle.

"Won't be long, sweetheart," she said, and turned again to me. "What do you think?" she asked me, very patiently.

I bit my lip hard.

"Not really sure?" she asked. "I don't blame you. I just had a thought. Some hospitals don't allow fresh flowers now, do they? Some new health and safety nonsense."

I stared at her and she nodded encouragingly. Giant hoop earrings jiggled beside her jaw.

"I think you should take fake ones." She beckoned to the reluctant sales assistant. "You got any silk flowers?"

The assistant discarded her headphones and moved silently into the dark little booth in the centre of the vast array of blooms. The girl took the empty carton of juice from the toddler and gave him a quick kiss.

I felt my brain beginning to reassemble itself. A decision had been made for me. My panic attack, if that's what it had been, was fading fast.

"These are nice." The assistant emerged with half an armful of beautiful silk flowers.

They were a mass of deep red, orange and purple. There were stocks in there, and gladioli, roses and zinnias. I thought of Vicky, in a hospital bed, sitting up and saying, "What? Fakes? Well, at least they can't die. Who's going to dust them?"

We'd laugh at that.

"Lovely," the girl was saying. "They look fantastic."

She watched over me as I paid, and put the handsome cardboard bag into my hand gently.

"Two minutes to go," she announced and turned the buggy round to head for the platform. "Platform fifteen."

In fact, the hospital where my sister was would have been very happy to accept real flowers. By the time I got there, Vicky was on a non-critical ward.

138

The Village

BEFORE we feel the winter chills
I'll go beyond the tumbling hills,
Down lanes which to a village wind,
Where folk are of the gentle kind.
A tranquil place, and there I'll see
A haven of antiquity.

There is a church of ancient date,
Quaint cottages that captivate.
An iron pump of vintage age
Beside the green, on centre stage.
And down a path a well, alone,
Can claim importance of its own.

And though all drudgery and tears
Belong back in the distant years,
The former school with silent bell
Must have some joyful tales to tell,
But keeps through every winter's blast,
The secrets of a misty past.

– Alice Jean Don.

She had suffered a serious reaction to a new chemical at work, completely unexpected. They said that it was lucky she came in so quickly because she needed all sorts of help to see her through it.

I don't know if the girl at the station thought that all hospitals ban flowers these days. I think she just said that in order to bring me round. She was passing in that place, so busy with life and people ignoring each other, and she noticed me, and stopped to help. There was even a chance that she might miss her train, looking after the mad woman at the florist's stand.

"So, not even real flowers?" Vicky asked as I approached her bed.

Her children parted like the Red Sea and Jonah grinned at me.

"You can wash them," I said, our eyes meeting. "Anyway, you've never thought of silk flowers. It shows ingenuity."

"Good choice, then. I just hope they fit in the washing machine."

I sat down on the chair by her bed.

"I had some help choosing them," I told her. "From a guardian angel at Victoria Station."

"You what?" Vicky asked, but then her youngest son began chattering, asking to go to the hospital shop for sweets.

"Oh," I said to no-one in particular, "it was one of those random acts of kindness." ■

Full Circle

by Sally Wragg.

THE surface of the lake glinted in the falling sun behind the vastness of Castle Keepsake. Kay Pritchard stood on the shore and allowed her gaze to come to rest on a swan that glided smoothly over the glass-like surface of the water. The sight was calming, lifting her spirits.

She'd felt unusually low on the long drive over here from Salford. She felt an affinity with the swans; so calm and serene on the surface, so much frenetic paddling underneath to keep afloat. Rather like herself, she mused.

The thought brought a smile to her face. It was a pretty face, though she didn't think so herself: a snub nose, deep-set, thoughtful eyes under a mass of hair the colour of spun gold. A serene expression belied the maelstrom of emotion beneath. Not even Denny, her friend, confidant and fellow student at university, had been able to discern the depth of her feelings.

"I can't seem to reach you, Kay, no matter how hard I try . . ." he'd said sadly when he finally broke off their relationship.

It was true. There was a part of herself she felt unable to share with anyone – even Denny, who had deserved so much more. He was a great guy and she was very fond of him, but she hadn't been able to love him. She'd even felt relief when he'd finally given up on her and found himself another girlfriend.

Time was pressing and, if she intended to return to her digs before dark, she would have to make a move back to her car, parked up by the castle. It had been a mistake to bolt back here, to Keepsake and the gamekeeper's cottage on the edge of the estate where she'd once lived with her father.

Sam Pritchard had long since moved away, his gamekeeping days behind him. The cottage they'd shared was occupied now by a young couple with a baby. She'd seen them in the garden and chatted a little when she'd passed by earlier. They seemed nice, but it was an odd feeling: the familiar little cottage

now home to strangers.

A cool breeze blew, rustling the leaves in the tangled shrubs and trees skirting the lake and almost obscuring the gazebo beyond. George, the old duke, would never have allowed them to grow out of control like this. He'd died last year, and Hugh, his son, had been forced back reluctantly from abroad to take up the mantle of the estate.

She really ought to go up to the castle and tell him she was here. She and Hugh had grown up together, roaming the grounds wherever the fancy took them. He'd be mortified to think she was here and hadn't called in to see him.

Seeing the gazebo brought back so many memories. Acting on impulse, she fought her way through the tangled mass of branches until she reached her goal, the dilapidated wooden structure whose dull ochre paint had peeled even more than she'd remembered. It had been their den, hers and Hugh's, the place to which they'd retreated whenever they were in trouble, which had been often enough. It had been the scene of picnics and midnight feasts and something else, too . . .

She stood, slightly breathless, looking about the place, redolent with the old, familiar musty smell of damp and mildew and late summer flowers. The scent brought back the memory of the day she'd told Hugh she was definitely taking up the place she'd been offered at university. He hadn't taken it well.

STUBBORN as ever, Hugh had greeted her news with the declaration that he would be moving abroad.

"What?" he'd cried. "You're not prepared to throw up everything and come with me? Kay! Whatever shall I do?"

He was trying to sound jokey and easy-going, but she could see by his expression that wasn't a bit how he felt. He would miss her, she knew that. What she really wanted was for him to tell her how much he'd miss her. She needed to know that his feelings for her were as strong as hers for him.

She stood, choked with emotions she'd no idea how to express. This time, even Hugh sensed that something was wrong.

His lips lifted into the old, familiar grin.

"It can't be helped. We'll work something out, Kay, don't worry."

She'd attempted a smile.

"We always knew it would happen some time."

"You go one way . . ."

"And you another," she finished for him.

There had been a pair of young swans on the lake, hardly out of their adolescent feathers, and she'd turned to watch them, if only to hide her pain. The male bird was paying court, but in such a desultory manner that she could see the female losing interest. It was obvious she'd had enough. Ruffling her feathers, turning full circle, she glided smoothly away. Her errant beau bowed his head and occupied himself with a series of unfocused pecks

142

around the edges of the lake.

But why hadn't he gone after her? Kay frowned, puzzled. Her head nodded towards the retreating swan, a huff of indignant feathers.

"She's left him. What a shame . . ."

"That's women for you," Hugh quipped. "It's what they all do in the end."

There was an edge to his voice she didn't quite like. Was he talking about her or the swan?

She frowned again.

"I have to do something with my life, Hugh. This course is just what I've been looking for. I'd be a fool to turn it down."

His shoulders lifted in apology.

"Of course you mustn't turn it down. I do understand, Kay. I know it's something you have to do. I thought you might have gone with your dad, though. I hadn't realised he was leaving the estate, too."

She nodded. Everything was changing. She had been sad to learn of her father's decision to leave Keepsake. He'd had enough of working on a big estate, he'd told her, and meant, with her approval, to try his hand at something else. Her connection with the castle would be gone once he moved.

"Dad's big enough and old enough to look after himself," she murmured. "Besides, he's with me all the way about university. He's always encouraged me to look forward. And what about you, Hugh? You can't mean to say your dad's keen on the idea of your swanning around Europe, doing nothing in particular? Aren't you supposed to stay here and show an interest in the estate?"

THE petulant scowl Hugh made in response had, unfortunately, become all too familiar to her. He'd sighed, thrusting his hands into his pockets and staring out moodily across the lake.

"A yoke around my neck whether I want it or not. Don't you see, Kay? I might as well enjoy myself now, while I can."

There was an awkward pause. She waited, hoping he might yet ask her to wait for him, tell her he'd wait for her . . .

"Life's too important to mess about, Hugh," she said gently.

"Isn't someone in my position supposed to do the grand tour?" he demanded.

"This is the twenty-first century, remember?" she scolded.

She stopped herself from going any further. Ancestral seats like Keepsake were kept going only by hard work performed by others for their owners. It crossed her mind that Hugh had always taken his privileged life for granted, whereas she, despite the idyllic nature of her existence here, had always known that, at some point, it would have to end. That point had been reached; much as she loved her father and their life here, she had to learn how to make a living for herself.

Camping Out

THEY say it's quite romantic
To sleep beneath the stars,
With a wise old owl keeping watch,
No noise, no passing cars.
But I wouldn't be too happy
Being inches off the ground
And when I fell asleep at night
Would those creatures run around?
Taking the wider view,
Of living and let live,
From them, I'd need some distance –
Something would have to give!
And then there's that equipment,
Bottled gas, so I could cook;
A night light for my reading,

For I'd just have to take that book.
It's the complete independence,
A "free spirit" holiday.
"We're all in this together!"
You hear them happily say.
But no, it doesn't tempt me,
Tho' the country I adore;
I'm attached to my home comforts,
To my polished parquet floor.
To my meals before the TV,
My pictures all around,
New kitchen and my own sweet bed
This is me – gone to ground!

– Dorothy McGregor.

This was truly the parting of the ways with Hugh. She couldn't bear to think of it.

Hugh's gaze had grown as troubled as hers.

"I'm going to miss you, Kay," he murmured.

She stood waiting in vain for him to say more, feeling as though her heart might burst.

"I shall miss you, too, Hugh," she answered. "But we'll keep in touch, won't we?"

"Of course we will!" he'd said vehemently.

A bird shrieked in the thicket, bringing Kay sharply back to the present. She recalled the fervour of that long-ago promise – a promise that had not been kept.

Kay had found it difficult to settle at university; it had been so different from anything she'd known before. Hugh, who had gone abroad almost as soon as she'd left, had seemed so far away. There had been a few snatched phone calls, of course, but as time went on, the duration of those calls became shorter and the space between them stretched from weeks to months.

Worse had been the awkward, stilted conversation at Hugh's father's funeral. Grief-stricken and surrounded by other members of his family, Hugh had seemed almost a stranger. She'd longed to comfort him, but he'd been so formal with her when they'd spoken. How could you comfort someone who

144

no longer cared for you?

He'd grown away from her; that much was clear.

She'd already met Denny by then. Perhaps Hugh had sensed that she was growing away, too.

Kay closed her eyes. Her hand rose to her cheek as if she could still feel the impression of Hugh's lips imprinted there at that final, bittersweet parting. It was as if they'd known, even then, that it was the parting of the ways . . .

"Kay? Is it really you?"

The voice breaking into her thoughts brought a gasp of joy to her lips. Hugh!

She jumped, swinging round towards him delightedly. She saw instantly that he'd changed, even since the funeral. He seemed older and conveyed some of the air of authority she remembered in his father. The impulse to throw her arms around him subsided.

"Josh – the guy who's taken over from your dad – said you'd been to the cottage . . ." he said. "I guessed you'd head straight here. You should have come up to the house, Kay. You were coming up to see me, surely?"

"Yes . . . no. Oh, Hugh, I'm not exactly sure!" She knew she sounded flustered. "I sort of wandered down here," she ended feebly.

"Why did you never keep in touch?" she burst out suddenly.

"*I* never kept in touch?"

He sounded oddly aggrieved.

She frowned.

"You didn't care!" she scolded him.

"You were too taken up with university," he returned.

"How would you know? You were never there!"

"Oh, but I was!"

This was news to Kay.

He grimaced, his gaze sliding from hers.

"I did visit you," he muttered. "I was back in England, visiting Father. I meant to surprise you. When I got to the university, someone told me you were in the student bar . . ."

"And?" she prompted.

"You were with someone else. You looked so happy."

"Denny," she murmured, feeling a pang of guilt.

"I left without saying anything – pretended I was never there."

"Hugh, I had a perfect right to see someone else. You should have told me you'd called!"

"And are you and he . . . together now?" he demanded.

She shook her head. Hugh's expression relaxed.

"You'll laugh," he said, "but, once upon a time, I used to think . . ."

His voice trailed away.

"What?" she implored.

"Nothing," he mumbled. "It's nothing. I just felt sad when I thought of how we used to be."

He was as hard to read as ever, but maturity had given Kay the wisdom to realise that what Hugh said didn't always match how he felt. Even so, she couldn't think what to say.

"Well, it's good to see you," she told him, inwardly cringing at how cowardly she was being.

"It's good to see you, too, Kay."

THE awkwardness had returned. This wasn't at all how she'd imagined the scene when she'd rehearsed their meeting. And she *had* rehearsed it, she realised now.

She had to accept it; it had been the chance of seeing Hugh again that had brought her rushing back here in the first place. When she'd arrived, it was only the anxiety about the reception she might receive that had prevented her going on up to the house.

The sun was sinking, a ball of molten fire reflected on the water sparkling through the trees. Time was pressing. It would be dark before long.

"You'll come up to the house?"

"I'm sorry, Hugh. I have to go."

His face softened.

"Please don't be sorry, Kay. I hate it when you're sorry."

She gazed up into his face. Was that merely fondness for an old friend she saw there or something more? How difficult it was to tell.

They began to make their way back to the lake, Hugh attempting to make conversation to fill the awkward gaps. He asked her about her time since university, and told her in return about his life on the estate – he was enjoying it more than he'd ever have believed possible.

A thorn snagged Kay's coat, but she scarcely noticed it, her mind was working so furiously. It was too long since they'd seen each other. Of course that accounted for all this ridiculous awkwardness. It felt so wrong, yet still she didn't know what to do.

"I'm parked back up at the castle," she told him, turning reluctantly for one last, lingering look at the lake.

A T that moment, a pair of swans floated into view from behind a clump of bulrushes. The sun bathed their downy feathers in rays of pink and gold. To her delight, as she watched, the male bird half rose, beating his wings across the surface of the water, sending a fine spray high into the air before he settled proudly back and lovingly twined his neck around his mate's.

At the sight, a memory stirred, bringing with it unexpected happiness. Surely it couldn't be . . .? But it was!

Kay gripped Hugh's arm.

"Those are our swans!" she exclaimed. "Look! He has a black mark on his beak whilst she . . ."

Could have been any swan, but Kay recognised her as the female who'd once rejected such an unworthy suitor. What had happened in the meantime? How had he managed to make her change her mind?

Suddenly, she knew exactly what had happened. Those silly birds had grown up, that was all!

Hugh appeared to have seen it, too. He laughed, the deep, rich laugh she'd not heard for too long.

"She finally knocked him into shape," he admitted.

She was filled with hope. Hugh had never wanted her to go away. She hadn't wanted to leave him. Life – and the fact that they'd both had a deal of growing up to do – had forced them apart.

He put his hands on her shoulders and turned her round gently to face him.

Kay's throat constricted, filled with an emotion she recognised at last – a little thing called love. I had always been there, but young and foolish as they'd been, it had been too much for them at the time.

"Hugh, I've missed you," she murmured.

"I've missed you, too, Kay," he said, and pulled her tenderly into his arms. ∎

Take A Chance On Me

By Patricia Clark.

YOU should have gone into service like your twin sisters, Millie and Kath," Mum said, not for the first time, as she took my supper out of the oven.

"I did warn you that shop work's not easy, even in a posh milliner's!"

I slipped off my shoes and stretched out my tired feet on the rag rug in front of the range.

"Come and sit at the table, Janet," Mum chivvied. "You'll feel better when you've some food inside you."

There wasn't much meat and even that was dried up as I'd been kept back with two difficult but important customers. They'd finally purchased two very expensive hats – one trimmed with mink, the other with ermine tails. No wonder Mrs Garner could afford her chauffeur-driven car!

"You could always leave, you know," Mum continued as she poured more gravy to moisten the meat. "Millie knows of a good place in Preston Park with the Ansell family where there are . . ."

She paused to think.

"Opportunities," she said finally, delighted to have lit on such an optimistic word.

But I wasn't impressed. Opportunities! To do what? Scrub and polish, fetch and carry. Slavery, that's what I called it. Not that I said as much to Mum as, sadly, that's what her life was.

Though I loved her dearly

148

and wanted to make her life better, at seventeen I knew what I wanted and it wasn't a job in service. Why did she have to keep mentioning it?

"You just want to let my room out, that's all," I blurted out crossly and, seeing the hurt in her tired eyes, instantly regretted it.

I leaned across the table and squeezed her hand.

"Sorry, Mum. I shouldn't have said that. I just prefer shop work and I'm determined to find the right place."

I struggled to cut through a tough piece of meat, and finally gave up, slipping it into my hankie when Mum wasn't looking. I didn't want to upset her any more, as money was tight since she'd been forced to give up her job as a bus conductress when the war ended and the returning men were given their jobs back.

We somehow got by on money from our lodger, Mr Early, a violinist at the Brighton Hippodrome, the contribution I gave her from my small wage, and her own earnings from a couple of cleaning jobs.

I remembered telling her once it wasn't fair.

"Dad didn't come back from the Somme, so why should you give up your job to someone who did?"

"Whoever said life was fair?" was her answer. "In many ways we are very fortunate. Remember that."

As I got up to wash my plate in the scullery, I relented.

"All right, Mum, I'll enquire at the Ansells' place when I can, I promise."

Her tired face brightened up and I decided with guilt that I would put her first for once, even though I really looked forward to enjoying the little free time I had.

The shop I worked in – Majestic Millinery – was in West Street, only a stone's throw from the sea. Whenever I had a chance, I would slip out, follow the cry of the seagulls, walk along the Prom past the posh hotels and then turn inland to my favourite place – Brighton Pavilion with its splendid domes like giant onions crowning the elegant white building.

THE day after I'd given my promise to Mum, Mrs Garner unexpectedly offered us an extra-long lunch break as she was giving a private viewing to some special friends. Betty, the other shop assistant, rushed out to find her fiancé while I walked down to the pier to catch a bus to Preston Park to check out the Ansells' position as I had promised Mum.

As I hurried along the street towards Harrington's Department Store, the sight of the stunning window models in the new-style chemises, soft and flowing – not a feather or corseted dress in sight – brought me to a sudden halt. So sudden, in fact, that Mr Early, our lodger, who happened to be walking in the same direction, banged into me, his violin case scraping the backs of my legs.

"I'm so sorry," he said, looking quite dapper in his evening suit. He made a performer's bow. "Not hurt, I hope. Our rehearsal has just finished so it's time for some refreshment before the matinée performance. Perhaps you'd like to join me?"

Before I could answer he shepherded me through the door. Everyone knew Harrington's, but the nearest I'd got to it was peering through the windows. Instinctively I knew I couldn't afford more than a card of plain buttons!

The warmth and brightness contrasted with the cold drab shop I worked in.

"Up we go!"

He stood back to let me in the lift first. It was an open cage, gold and ornate, and seemed to sum up the atmosphere of the whole store – an Aladdin's cave, bright and exciting.

"I wish I worked here," I told him, as he poured out the tea the waitress had promptly brought, obviously recognising him as a regular. "The fashions are so beautiful and modern."

"What's wrong with Majestic Milliners?"

"Everything!"

He laughed and encouraged me to go on. I felt so grown-up having tea with a professional musician who was treating me with kindness. It was less

150

The Eden Project

DEEP in the heart of Cornwall, the Eden Project sits in the footprint of a clay pit that was in use for over 160 years. The idea for its creation came from the mind of Tim Smit, a Dutch-born British businessman who was involved in the regeneration of the popular Lost Gardens of Heligan.

Inspired by his experience to create a showcase of the world's most important plants, he came up with the idea for the Eden Project. The giant bubble design – the signature biomes of the Project – was later developed by the architectural firm involved, and constructed using a world-record-setting 230 miles of scaffolding!

Plants from all over the world now draw visitors from far and wide, and the Project receives visits from schools, gets involved in community work, hosts creative events and provides valuable working positions for the unemployed and homeless. Much more than just a pretty garden!

151

stilted than when we met at home – which was rarely because of the odd hours he worked.

I took a bite of the madeleine he offered me, a tiny sponge pyramid coated with jam and dusted with coconut, knowing I'd remember it for ever. Then I launched into a list of my complaints.

"First, there's Mrs Garner's snooty attitude. She treats Betty and me like slaves, expecting us to work extra hours for no extra pay." I paused to take another bite of my cake and a sip of tea out of the bone china cup.

"Secondly, her hats are so old-fashioned, the same styles as before the war. Apart from what they look like, lots of those feathers come from rare birds of paradise. One customer told me that it took the death or wounding of these young exotic birds to create a hat. Then she walked out saying it was disgusting. Not that Mrs Garner believed me. She said I was making excuses for an unsuccessful sale!"

"I may have the answer," Mr Early interrupted and poured some more tea. "There was an advertisement in yesterday's 'Evening Argus' for a vacancy here in Haberdashery," he said.

"Buttons, elastic, braid and ribbons!" I chanted, already imagining cutting off lengths, advising customers on the right ribbons for a garment or hat, and, at the end of the day, making sure my counter was clean and polished and the contents of the glass-fronted drawers neat and tidy.

"That's it and more." He nodded and clasped his hands. "Now it's up to you. Go to the department on the ground floor and ask for details. They will probably ask if you want to live in."

This last piece of news was the icing on the cake. A job in Harrington's and I could live in, meaning Mum could take in another lodger and cut down on the cleaning jobs that were wearing her out.

"Thank you, Mr Early."

I jumped up, and to his obvious embarrassment, kissed him firmly on the cheek.

I plucked up courage to speak to a very glamorous woman at the Haberdashery counter. She looked very sophisticated but her friendly approach put me at ease. I was soon telling her about my experience at the shop and how much I would like the job.

"So at Majestic Millinery you decorate hats with different ribbons and chiffon flowers to suit the individual's taste? That's good experience for helping customers in this department. You must have an eye for colour and shape, of course."

"I like to think so," I said, encouraged by her tone. "There are some things that trouble me at Mrs Garner's, though," I ventured.

"Can you tell me what?" Again the encouraging tone, as if she were really interested in my opinions.

"The feathers that she insists people want. It seems so cruel."

"I couldn't agree more." The assistant smiled. "Thank goodness they are going out of fashion. The new cloche hats are exciting, don't you think?" she asked.

"Like on the models, you mean? The colours are beautiful and so flattering to the face, and the tight fit shows off the features really well."

She nodded.

"Your enthusiasm for fashion is obvious and haberdashery is a good place to start if you are interested in progressing in a department store. Hand in a letter of application as soon as you can after opening tomorrow. And good luck!"

I was in a dream as I left the shop and turned down towards the sea to think things over. The wind was even fresher than before, the breakers crashing on the shingle under the pier, but it all added to my exhilaration. Even the diving seagulls seemed to be squawking congratulations. For I really felt I had been promised the job and that all I had to do was submit my letter in my best handwriting.

* * * *

Back at the shop I couldn't stop smiling as I told Betty all about my good fortune. She was really happy for me, I could tell.

"I'm sure you'll get the job," she said. "But wait till it's all done and dusted, though, before you tell Mrs Garner."

Dear kindly, down-to-earth Betty. I would miss working with her.

"We can meet at lunch breaks," I told her.

"'Course we can."

I SUPPPOSE I was still smiling when I turned into our street and met Mrs Wilson, the local gossip.

"Hello," I greeted her brightly. "How are you today?"

"I'm quite well, thank you," she snapped. "It's your mother you should be worried about. I've just been talking to her and she'll soon wipe that smile off your face, you little madam," she finished with a smirk and bustled off, no doubt to spread more mischief.

Mum was in the scullery washing up the teacups and plates from the visit.

"Everything all right?" I put my arms round Mum's waist. I couldn't wait to tell her my news, but I could tell Mrs Wilson had upset her because she hadn't looked round when I came in.

She put down the dishcloth and turned, not a flicker of a smile on her normally happy face.

"I'm disappointed, that's all, if what Mrs Wilson told me is true."

It turned out Mrs Wilson had been shopping in North Street and had seen Mr Early ushering me into Harrington's.

"I won't repeat the names she called you," she said, picking up the tea cloth. "I know you wouldn't do anything improper." She bit her lip. "But you did promise that if you had any time off you'd at least go and find out about the Ansells' position."

My heart sank. I felt so guilty.

"I forgot, I'm sorry, Mum. I did intend to. After Mrs Garner gave us a long lunch break I was on the way to the bus stop when I stopped to look in Harrington's window. Mr Early bumped into me and when I tell you that I might have a better job, I know you'll be pleased."

Mum softened a little.

"Go on then, tell me all about it." At last she smiled. "Every detail, mind!"

And I did.

"I got on really well with the lady in charge in Haberdashery," I finished, trying to explain why she made me feel so confident of success. "I really want to work there, Mum."

"Of course you do. Make a good job of that letter and I'm sure you'll be successful."

"If I do, I'll owe Mr Early a big thank-you," I said. "He's a nice man, Mum,

Autumn Twilight

So softly falls the dusk, now autumn's here,
And though we sigh as precious daylight wanes,
There's something friendly in the atmosphere.
As lamps gleam out from countless window-panes.
And nature seems, as evening shadows fall,
To wrap her gentle arms round one and all.

The moon-white daisies tremble in the breeze,
A barn-owl hoots and pale moths flutter by,
All hushed and silent are the ancient trees,
While in the dreamy purple of the sky,
Soon, the first star of evening will appear
So small, so welcome, shining crystal clear.

And this I know, as scents of autumn drift,
Over quiet meadows veiled in amethyst,
That in such peaceful places still abide
Spirits of those who loved the countryside.

– *Kathleen O'Farrell.*

Thinkstockphotos.

and kind like Uncle Bert was – and Dad, of course."

"Yes, he is, almost a lost generation," Mum said sadly.

A LOST generation." I lay in bed thinking of Mum's words. No wonder she looked after Mr Early so well; he was one of the survivors to cherish. She often waited up late to make sure he had a hot drink when he came in after an evening performance at the Hippodrome.

Sometimes I could hear the murmur of their chatter as I lay in bed. I liked that, as it reminded me of simpler childhood days when Mum and Dad did the same. I realised as never before how I missed Dad and the blanket of security he and Mum had surrounded me with.

That night I couldn't sleep, partly because Mum still hadn't cheered up and partly due to the excitement at the possibility of a job in Harrington's. It must have been gone 11 when I heard Mr Early come in. I heard the clattering of the pan of milk on the range to warm.

The usual murmur of voices wasn't enough for me. I wanted to hear what they were saying, guessing they might talk about me, curious what they would say. So I crept to the door, gingerly opened it and stood at the top of the stairs.

I couldn't make out every word, but I worked out they were talking about me and Harrington's. Imagining Mr Early putting in a good word for me gave me a nice feeling. But then the friendly tones were suddenly interrupted by Mum. Not that she shouted, but her voice was firm and clear.

"It's not your place, Ernest, to encourage my daughter to leave home. I'll always want her here till she gets married, whatever you say about it."

Dismayed, I crept back into bed. So Mr Early had told her about the chance of my living in at Harrington's and she clearly didn't approve. Half of me wanted to march downstairs and have it out with them, the other half thought I might make matters worse. And that half won.

B LEARY-EYED from a poor night's sleep, and determined to have it out with her, I faced Mum over the breakfast table as I finished my porridge.

"I couldn't help hearing what you said last night," I began, "when you were talking to Mr Early about me leaving home."

"Nothing for you to worry about," she said briskly. "If you get the job – and, as I said last night, I hope you do – and you want to live in, that's all right. But I don't want you to go just because –" she paused and then went on, almost spitting out the words with scorn "– just because our lodger suggests it!"

Pouring out the tea gave her time to think and calm down a bit.

"It's Mr Early I'm cross with, not you. Let's wait and see if you get the job and then the two of us will talk about it."

"Thanks, Mum."

For once she was really treating me like a grown-up.

"You're my daughter and very special," she went on, "and always will be even if Ernest –" She stopped and picked up the empty bowls, taking them out to the scullery. "I've told Mr Early to start looking for some new lodgings," she muttered and refused to elaborate further. It seemed a bit extreme, for the man was only trying to help, but what could I do?

At Harrington's I handed in my letter and was asked to call back after work.

"You've already had an interview with Miss Vine," the receptionist in the office said. "Yes, she's written quite a detailed appraisal," she added with a smile as she riffled through some papers.

I longed to ask if there were many other applicants but didn't dare.

* * * *

At work I upset Mrs Garner by breaking two feathers when I dropped a hat when making a window display. I couldn't concentrate when so much was going round in my head. Would I get the job I wanted so badly? If I did, what could I do about Mum's falling out with Mr Early? I knew she liked his company and he'd been so helpful to me.

"You're her last daughter at home," Betty reminded me. "She's bound not to like a stranger advising you."

I told her that "Ernest", as she called him, was hardly a stranger, but I did see her point.

"WELCOME aboard," Miss Vine greeted me as I stepped through the shop door. She shook my hand warmly. "I'm off to a meeting now," she added, "so I can't stop. Call at the office and collect your offer of appointment, the terms and conditions and commencement date.

"One thing more, if you were expecting to live in I'm afraid that won't be possible at the moment. All staff quarters are full. I hope that's not a problem."

"Not at all," I said, and then she was gone.

Outside in the street I felt like shouting my joy to the rooftops. Instead, not wanting to appear a mad woman by anyone inside Harrington's, I raced down to the sea front and on to the shingle and threw a few pebbles into the foam to get rid of all that energy and excitement.

Mr Early was far from my thoughts, I must admit, until I reached home to be greeted by a murmur of voices drifting into the hall as I opened the front door. I knew it was Mum and Mr Early.

Then suddenly a loud shriek came from Mum as I turned the doorknob to push open the kitchen door. They were standing by the table with their backs to me, unaware of my presence. And they were laughing now, staring at a large iced cake that had somehow fallen off the plate on to the cloth. It was all so bizarre. I just stood there and watched like a spectator in the theatre, waiting for the next move.

"So that's what you think of my peace offering and my proposal?" he teased.

"We'll be able to save most of it. It was such a surprise and so beautiful. How could I let it slip from my hand?" Mum touched him gently on the arm and reached over to the cutlery basket, preparing to scoop it up. And that's when she noticed me.

"Janet!" She blushed, her eyes sparkling as she looked back at Mr Early. "I didn't hear you come in. We were –"

"No need to explain, Mum. I think I've got the picture. Mr Early's staying, I imagine, and . . ."

"I've asked your mother to marry me," he put in.

"And I've accepted," she finished.

"And I've promised not to forget how important you are to her," he said, squeezing her hand.

"He means that your place is here with us for as long as you want. I nearly forgot, how did you get on at Harrington's? Did you hand in your letter?"

"I did." I tried my best to look downcast. "But they don't want to interview me."

At the sight of their shocked faces I laughed.

"They said I didn't need a proper interview after my conversation yesterday. I have the position!"

Mum flung her arms round me as Mr Early dished out the crumbly celebration cake and opened the bottle of sherry kept for special occasions.

After all the toasts I told them, "There isn't any spare accommodation at Harrington's – and I really only wanted it so you could get another lodger. But when you two are married there will be room for another lodger."

"There'll be no need for another lodger, will there, Ernest?" Mum nodded to him. "Tell her your good news."

"We will have more money than we thought," he said, putting his arm gently round Mum's shoulders. "I've been promoted to First Violinist at the Hippodrome." He coughed. "It's quite an honour and an increase in salary."

"That's brilliant, Mr –"

"Call me Ernest, please," he insisted.

"So when Millie and Kath come to visit I won't have to sleep on the sofa. I can't wait till Christmas."

My mind was leaping ahead, imagining us all sitting round the table, Mum bringing in the Christmas pudding, Ernest pouring brandy over it and lighting it and my older sisters passing round the plates.

"There will be room for everyone." ■

Come All Ye Faithful

WHEN Clarissa Bollington-Smythe clapped her hands, everyone stopped talking and paid attention.

What a wonderful woman, Frank thought. How many people could do that?

"Does everyone have lyric sheets?" she boomed.

They all nodded, apart from Stan the printer, who was wondering how he had been persuaded to supply so many copies for free. The owner of his own print shop and pillar of the community, he also printed the parish magazine, but he sometimes felt there were certain people who didn't realise he had a business to run.

One of the children put up his hand.

"Yes, Peter?"

By Rebecca Holmes.

"Some of these carols are new, Mrs B. We don't know them."

Several older members of the group tutted at this and raised their eyebrows.

"On the contrary, Peter, they're traditional." Clarissa raised her eyes heavenwards. "Aren't these fine old songs sung at school any more?"

Jenny Carr, an infants' teacher at the local primary school, said nothing. Having only started in September, and being new to the area, she didn't feel ready to take on well-established locals yet, especially ones with double-barrelled surnames.

"You'll soon get the hang of them," the double-barrelled name was saying now. "Just listen to everyone else and mime if you're stuck."

Marvellous woman, Frank said to himself. If only there were more like her . . .

And if only she'd notice him more. He might have been the gardener at the Grange for nearly 15 years, starting back when Mr Bollington-Smythe had been alive, and they might see each other practically every day, but in many ways they were worlds apart.

Their little group of about 20 carol singers had become something of a highlight over the years. Of course, people came and went, but it was generally accepted that this annual traditional would carry on no matter what else might change. And change there had been aplenty in their small market town, including a giant new supermarket and the housing estate they were visiting now.

Tonight was perfect – a proper, crisp December evening, with frost already sparkling on the pavements. Thousands of stars glinted in the sky and everyone's breaths formed little clouds.

"We'll start with 'Silent Night'."

The singers were just clearing their throats, when another sound assaulted the still night air.

"Good heavens!" Clarissa exclaimed. "What on earth's that racket?"

"It's Slade, Mrs B.," Peter said.

"Slayed? It certainly should be slayed, if you ask me! The point is, what's it doing here?"

EVERYONE looked round to see where the loud music was coming from. Frank clapped his hand to his forehead.

"The Rotary Club! I forgot they were doing their Santa's Sleigh Run tonight."

Clarissa frowned.

"But it's Tuesday. I thought they did Little Crimping then."

"They did. But some people complained they were being left out, so they've rearranged their schedule to fit more places in."

Even as he spoke, a tractor rounded the bend, pulling a trailer flanked by chipboard that had been shaped and painted to resemble the sides of a sleigh, and

159

edged with coloured lights. Perched on top, next to an enormous speaker, sat "Santa", who looked as if he'd lost weight since last year – probably because he was a different person.

Frank groaned inwardly as he recognised the owner of the new organic shop from just down the road. The man had become a regular visitor to the Grange, delivering a weekly box even though they had a perfectly good vegetable plot.

Volunteers carrying buckets and wearing reflective jackets were already ringing doorbells. It didn't take a genius to work out that a second collection, from their little group, wouldn't be so welcome.

"How can we compete with Father Christmas?" someone at the back asked.

Some of the smaller children started crying.

Clarissa sighed heavily.

"Now what?"

Jenny bent down and listened as her young pupils told her their woes.

"Hannah and Katie are worried they'll miss Father Christmas," she explained, straightening up. "If this one hasn't seen them at home tonight, he might tell the real one they've moved and they won't be left any presents."

Clarissa's face softened.

Not just wonderful, but warm-hearted, too, Frank thought.

"Don't worry. We'll have a chat with Santa to put him right."

SQUARING her shoulders, she strode off, the two little girls following in her wake. Over the years, Frank had come to recognise a certain look about her whenever she meant business. She was wearing that look now. From the way young Jack Brown, driving his father's tractor, was gripping the steering wheel, Frank didn't doubt that he'd recognised it, too.

Jenny was also watching the proceedings with interest, and not just on Hannah and Katie's behalf. She, too, had noticed Jack, and her heart lifted at the sight of a friendly face. When she'd moved into her flat, he'd popped round to welcome her and ask whether she wanted milk delivered from Brown's Dairy, with a special rate for the first two weeks.

She had been interested anyway, but his warm, open smile had clinched the deal. It seemed such a pity that they were on opposing sides tonight, so to speak.

After a few minutes, Frank shifted his weight from one foot to the other. The lady couldn't be losing her touch, could she?

A sudden thought hit him. Only this afternoon, he'd seen "Father Christmas" carry an enormous turkey into the Grange, and spend quite a while there before finally driving off. Now here he was again, too smooth by half, and deep in conversation with Clarissa. This didn't look good. It didn't look good at all.

Fifty Years Ago . . .

November 2, 1964.

WHEN the doors of the Crossroads Motel opened to the viewing public, few could have predicted how popular this TV series would become. Featuring the redoubtable Noele Gordon as motel owner Meg Richardson, "Crossroads" was set in fictional Kings Oak on the outskirts of Birmingham.

With a tiny budget and limited filming time, the soap opera was ridiculed for its wobbly scenery and fluffed lines but soon established itself in the hearts of the British viewing public and at times beat "Coronation Street" into second place in the viewing figures.

Storylines could be controversial for the time and included Meg's son, Sandy, being paraplegic and in a wheelchair, the first time a main character had been portrayed this way.

The soap opera originally ran five nights a week, eventually dropping to three. It ended in 1988 and was briefly revived three years later to run for another two years before finally coming to an end.

161

Clarissa's stride on her return journey wasn't so purposeful, though at least Katie and Hannah looked reassured.

"There's been a change of plan," she announced, as everyone strained to hear her over Shakin' Stevens. "It would be ridiculous for both sets of us to go round the same houses, so we'll cover the larger, outlying residences and then maybe some of the pubs. It may involve a little more leg work, but I'm sure we'll all find it an interesting experience."

Some of the children's eyes lit up at the prospect of going farther afield. And after dark, too.

And why not, Frank thought. It is Christmas, after all.

It also meant they wouldn't have to join forces with Santa's Sleigh Run.

✳ ✳ ✳ ✳

Two hours later, the exhausted but happy troupe sang their last carol – "God Rest Ye Merry, Gentlemen" – at the Royal Oak. Gossip circulated round the room. Hadn't it been nice of Mrs Morris at Honeysuckle Cottage to hand out all those mince-pies? The Vicarage was generally agreed to be in need of a lick of paint, which was a shame, as the vicar was such a lovely man. And Mrs Watkins would have no problem finding homes for Mitzi's kittens, now everyone had fallen in love with them.

It had been quite an evening for the children, too, going round the "posh" houses and the sort of pubs that were normally the grown-ups' domain. Not only that, but they were about to be bought all the cola and lemonade they could drink and crisps they could eat.

Peter had learned lots of new carols, and planned to sing every one of them to his mum tomorrow evening when she iced the cake. Katie and Hannah were busy watching Stan, who was showing them card tricks.

AT the polished wooden bar, Frank and Clarissa counted out the mountains of change, and even notes, that had been stuffed in the collection bags. They may not have been rattling buckets, but they'd still collected a sizeable amount, which the local hospice would put to good use.

The place deserved every penny, in Frank's view, especially after looking after his Emily so well during the last weeks of her illness. It had been an inspired idea of Clarissa's to change tactics tonight, just as it had been her idea to start up the carol singing to raise money for the hospice after Emily's death.

"I know what it's like to lose someone," she'd said at the time. "And it'll give you a sense of purpose to help keep you going."

Suddenly the door opened and the rotary club volunteers streamed in. There were waves and good-natured greetings all round, any former rivalry forgotten as everyone bought everyone else drinks. Only Frank stiffened.

There was no sign of "Organic Man", but he was bound to be somewhere. He nudged one of the members standing nearby.

"Where's Father Christmas?"

"Alastair? Oh, he's gone home. He's got an early start tomorrow, going up to meet his fiancée's parents. He was quite nervous about it, actually. It seems the prospective mother-in-law's a bit of a dragon." He chuckled. "Still, I suppose at his age he can't afford to be too fussy."

If anything further was said, it was lost amid the cheering as Clarissa made her announcement of the grand total collected. Frank cheered, too, and not just about the amount raised.

Tucked away in a quiet corner, Jenny joined in, but she couldn't help feeling left out. Naturally, she'd enjoyed doing her bit, and everyone here was friendly enough in their own way, but now they all seemed to be settled in

Barra

T HE garden of the Western Isles,
Surrounded by the wild North Sea,
Was where, one day, I stepped ashore
And now its magic follows me.
It seems wherever I might go,
I see its marsh and moorland ways,
And heather, where the land is bare,
Appears reflected in my gaze.

Orchid, primrose, celandine,
Continually are brought to mind,
As if, upon that fateful day,
I left the world I knew behind.
Barra waits for spring's return,
To wash it free from winter's stain,
But most of all, it calls to me,
To venture to its shores again.

Island daughter of the sea,
Of songs that float on wind and wing,
Of purple dawns and sunsets gold,
Where seal pups bask and wild winds sing;
A garden floating in the mist,
Of croft and loch and rolling hill;
It calls me back to live the dream,
I must return. One day I will.

– Dawn Lawrence.

their own little huddles.

If only she wasn't so shy. She could manage a class of infants, so why not this? Maybe she should just go home, and try to get to know people more gradually, when she wasn't so tired and they weren't so busy.

She picked up her bag, preparing to leave, when someone tapped her shoulder. There, smiling broadly, was Jack.

Well, that was the evening almost over, Frank thought. People were starting to drift away. It was now or never. He took a deep breath.

"Could I have the pleasure of buying you a glass of wine?" he asked Clarissa.

She beamed at him.

"Thank you, Frank. That sounds like a very good idea."

Even if the Royal Oak had fallen down around their ears, nothing could have taken anything away from how Frank felt at that moment. So far as he was concerned, everything he wanted for Christmas was right here, and there was no Santa Claus in sight! ■

Ever-changing Patterns

A KALEIDOSCOPE of patterns
Now adorns my window-pane.
This wondrous sight of sheer delight,
Entices me again.

Without the aid of stencils
To form these works of art,
As nature planned, she lent her hand,
Though unseen, played her part.

Outside, the grass now spiked with white,
Presents a sparkling scene,
For icy dew has changed the view –
I can but stare and glean.

For overnight Jack Frost appeared,
Though failed to get inside
To decorate my window-pane,
Although he might have tried!

I caught him early morning
On the outside, looking in,
At every turn, so he could learn
From spiders, how they spin!

– *Joan Zambelli.*

Thinkstockphotos.

Dundee

BONNIE Dundee, home of "The People's Friend", is a small city that nestles on the banks of the Tay as it turns from river to estuary and runs into the North Sea. Its setting was once described by Stephen Fry, a former Rector of the University of Dundee, as "about as ideal as any city setting could be".

Once the proud home of the three "J"s – jam, jute and journalism – Dundee is undergoing something of a rebirth after the wane of its key industries. It's now home to thriving computing and scientific industries, as well as a burgeoning arts scene – soon to be complemented by the opening of a branch of the Victoria & Albert museum.

Although the city is changing fast, and new structures are going up as quickly as the old ones – like these now-vanished blocks of flats – are coming down, the city centre is still small enough to be easily accessible to visitors. And, in spite of all the changes, it's still home to a journalist or two!

Wish Upon A Star

by Marilyn Fountain.

IT'S no good, Julie," Tim's muffled voice called down from the loft, "it's definitely not here."

With reluctance, Julie mounted a couple of rungs up the stepladder. A rush of cold air touched her face and the musty aroma prickled the back of her throat.

"It must be, Tim. Where else would we have put it?"

Julie thought back to early autumn when they'd moved into Bay House. It had enough cupboards and cubby holes for everyday stuff, so only the rarely used items were bundled up to the loft. And it was here they'd always kept the funny old artificial Christmas tree and all its decorations in the past.

Julie physically ached when she thought of their old home and its wealth of happy memories. If only she could turn back the clock to last Christmas, with her mum there and their son, Tate, still living at home.

A thud and a muttering from above forced Julie up another step.

"Tim, are you all right?"

"Fine, love. Apart from nearly putting my foot through the ceiling, that is." Her husband's dust-covered face emerged over the side of the hatch. "I've just found a box of old paperbacks. Do you want them while I'm up here?"

Julie was unsure. She couldn't settle to reading lately, or anything else for that matter. This was a year she wouldn't be sad to see the back of. So many changes, and none of them for the better. Losing Mum so unexpectedly in the summer was the worst. They were already committed to buying Bay House at the time, because it had an extra downstairs room, ideal so Mum could move in with them. But it wasn't meant to be.

Then Tate had got the opportunity of a teaching job in the Far East. Julie was thrilled for him, but missed him desperately. The new house just didn't feel like home. With Tate not being able to get back for Christmas, Julie had already been half-hearted about trimming up. And now the decorations had been mislaid, it seemed like the final straw.

"Julie! These books . . .?"

"Yes, please, Tim," she suddenly decided. "You might as well bring them down."

If the stories didn't capture her imagination, they'd be better off going to the charity shop so someone else could benefit from them.

BACK down in the kitchen, with Tim inspecting his stubbed toe, Julie thumbed through the books while the kettle boiled. She was still mulling over where the tree might be. Apparently, so was her husband.

"I know what could have happened to the Christmas stuff," Tim said. "It might have been shipped to the charity shop by mistake, along with all the other stuff we cleared out when we moved."

Julie gazed at him in dismay. All the decorations couldn't be lost, surely?

The threadbare little folding tree that her mum and dad had bought when they first married, and the box of decorations they'd accumulated as a family through the years, were like a time capsule of seasonal memories, a part of her childhood and adult life. Even if she wasn't going to use them this year, the idea they were still with her was a comfort.

"We're going to have to buy new, then," Tim said.

Julie stared at her husband, sipping his tea as if nothing was wrong. She thumped her mug on the table.

"I don't want new. It won't be the same. I don't think we should bother trimming up this horrible house, anyway. With Tate away and Mum gone, what's the point?"

"Well, you still have me, love . . ."

His tone was light, but the forlorn sentiment struck a nerve. Julie knew she was being a right selfish pain, and how bad that was making Tim feel she couldn't begin to imagine.

"I'm sorry, Tim. I know I'm so blessed to have you . . ." she began, holding out her hand to him, and then suddenly she was crying again.

Tim stumbled to his feet, tripping over his discarded trainers, and came round to her side of the table to wrap his arms around her.

"Give the house time, love," he soothed. "I know we wouldn't have moved at all if we hadn't thought your mum would be coming here with us, but we're here now, so we might as well make the best of it."

She clung to him, grateful for his support.

December

IN winter we go whole days without seeing light –
The trees condemned, heads bowed and bare.

Except for the odd pale yellow window,
Sky and hills and woods are one, grey and dead.

Hard to believe there will be daffodils,
That green things will happen again.

At night, houses shine out in cries across fields of
    floodwater,
The cold of wet and wind like the cut of a spade in
    bare hand.

We pull our hopes and dreams behind us on
    sledges
Into the sheer hope of light, the one clenched
    promise of spring.

– Kenneth Steven.

"I know," she murmured, "I know . . ." Saying it, however, was one thing, believing it was something else.

"And we want the house to look nice when we Skype Tate on Christmas Day, don't we?" Tim said. "I'll set up the laptop so he'll be able to see the tree behind us."

Would their son notice a different tree and decorations, she wondered, or would he be too caught up with his new life?

"I'll pick up a tree on the way home from work tomorrow, Julie, if you want to choose some new decorations next time you're in town?"

∗　∗　∗　∗

I've got it!" Tim's excited face peered around the kitchen door the following evening.

Julie looked up, wondering why he wasn't bringing the box straight in.

"It's a bit larger than I planned, but I saw it and just sort of fell in love with it." He grinned, then turned and started pulling it through the door.

"But it's a real one!" she exclaimed, as first a mass of roots and then a column of green appeared.

It stretched from one side of the kitchen cabinets to the other. Julie stared at it warily before looking at Tim.

"What on earth made you get a real tree?"

"It was the last one for sale from a chap on the roundabout, and I felt a bit sorry for it . . ." he admitted sheepishly.

She couldn't help but smile at his soft heart.

"I can see why it was the last one," she said. "It's not very straight, is it?"

"Perhaps it'll look better when it's upright."

"If it'll go upright," she considered, eyeing the ceiling height. "And we've got to find something to put it in."

Tim unearthed an old dustbin from round the back of the shed, and with the light spilling on to the garden from the open kitchen door, they could see just enough to dig up some soil.

"We've never had a real tree before," Julie said, as they arranged the roots to fit. "These seem very dry. I'm not sure if it's going to survive."

"We'll give it plenty of water and wish very hard." Tim grinned.

His cheeks were flushed from digging, and Julie thought how happy he looked.

Eventually they managed to manoeuvre the tree into the corner of the conservatory.

"I'll twirl it round until we find the best side," Tim said.

"I'm not sure it's got one!" she murmured.

"There!" Tim stepped back to admire the effect. "All it needs now is decorating and a bright set of lights."

Julie wondered if its droopy branches would bear the weight of plastic baubles, let alone a heavy string of lights. Still, it would get them through Christmas week, and then they could throw it out, she thought, as she turned to sweep up the trail of dirt and dropped needles.

In the morning, she peeped through the glass door to the conservatory. The tree was still upright, though looking distinctly sorry for itself.

"Just try to hang on for a few days," she told it briskly.

The shop windows in town were as shiny and festive as ever, but Julie felt too flat to be cheered by them. The Salvation Army band playing in the shopping centre brought a lump to her throat. She and her mum had always come into town on Christmas Eve to listen to the carols.

Pausing only to push a few coins in the donations tin, Julie passed on, heading for the charity shop. She'd brought a carrier bag full of the paperbacks to donate.

There was a modern artificial tree in the charity shop window, surrounded by candles, tinsel and small wooden toys. Wouldn't it be a miracle, Julie thought, if their old tree was inside for sale?

But the assistant on duty told her apologetically that any trees they'd been given had been snapped up weeks ago.

"Not to worry," Julie replied, and related the circumstances. "I'm not even sure if it came here. It could have been left in the back of the furniture van, or put out with the rubbish."

"Aw, it's a shame, though," the assistant sympathised. "We've a few mixed decorations if you need any."

Julie riffled through the box of remaining odds and ends. At the bottom was a familiar item, the old silver star that had always dressed the top of their tree. She pressed it to her chest and felt tears prick her eyelids.

"At least it proves the tree and decorations did come here rather than end on the council tip."

She must have spoken her thoughts aloud because the assistant replied, "Your tree will have raised much-needed funds, and I'm sure it'll have gone to a good home."

Julie decided there was comfort to be drawn from knowing that their old family tree was now a part of someone else's special Christmas. And, at the end of the day, she had the silver star. One small but precious part of the past to hold on to – and to try to brighten up the poor old replacement lurking in the corner of the conservatory. Now all she had to do was find a mountain of tinsel and some featherweight lights to disguise the rest of its dishevelled state.

WITH just a week until Christmas Day, Julie lavished attention on the tree, watering it daily.

"Here you are," she told it, adding to the watering can some special liquid plant food she'd got from the garden centre, "this might perk you up a bit. When I was a girl my mum gave me a spoonful of sticky syrup called Virol

Fifty Years Ago . . .
November 27, 1964.

WHEN the Beatles had their third No. 1 of the year with "I Feel Fine", it rounded off quite a year for the four from Liverpool. Earlier they had hits with "Can't Buy Me Love" and "A Hard Day's Night" and their film of the same name was released in July showing the lads in a mock documentary.

The beginning of this year had seen them enter the US Billboard Magazine charts and in February they visited the USA to be met with hordes of screaming fans at Kennedy Airport. Their performance on the Ed Sullivan Show broke all viewing records and they were quickly invited back.

Within a short time Billboard was reporting that the Beatles' records held 14 positions on the Top 100 Chart, beating the previous record set by Elvis Presley. Meanwhile, in Australia, they were to occupy the top six positions.

Their year came to a close with "I Feel Fine" still holding the No. 1 spot at Christmas.

to buck me up and get me through the winter . . ."

Julie was only glad Tim wasn't around to witness her talking to a fir tree. He'd think she'd really lost the plot. Whether it was the plant food, the good talking-to, or just wishful thinking, she thought the tree might be responding. The needles seemed a brighter green, and the stem was firm enough to support the treasured family star.

She was particularly pleased with the candle-shaped set of lights she'd found to go on it, along with some pretty glass decorations. And, continuing the natural theme, she added pine cones and sprigs of holly.

"There!" she said, standing back to gauge the effect. "Not too bad at all." She stroked the branches, and far fewer needles than usual fell off.

* * * *

Switching on the lights on Christmas Eve was poignant, because her mum had always done that. Julie closed her eyes and let Tim do the honours.

"Hey! It's great!" he exclaimed.

Julie opened her eyes. Yes, it did look good. Even if it wasn't their familiar old tree standing in the corner of their old living-room by the fireplace, she could get used to it.

Rain started to splatter on the conservatory roof.

"Doesn't look as if we'll be having a white Christmas," Tim remarked.

"Is it me, or can you hear singing?" She blinked.

It was carol singers coming down the path. Julie ran to open the door to a group of a dozen adults, teenagers and children.

"You can't stand out there in this weather," Tim said, ushering them all inside.

Julie was glad she'd made some mince-pies. She set them in the oven to warm while the singers gathered in the conservatory. As they softly sang, "O, Christmas Tree", Julie held her breath and let the magic wash over her. It had been her mum's favourite carol.

"That was really beautiful," she told Tim, wiping her eyes after their unexpected visitors had gone. "I think it's just made my Christmas."

"You've still got your present to come tomorrow." Tim's eyes twinkled as he gave her a hug.

He was more of a big kid than Tate had ever been when it came to Christmas. Despite her earlier misgivings, she felt she'd done the right thing in celebrating the season after all. She laughed, and Tim hugged her harder.

"What's that for?" she asked breathlessly.

"Because it's lovely to hear you laugh again."

She leaned back to look at him, and it suddenly dawned on her. His support for her, all the while she'd been grieving, had been patient and unwavering. A part of her had been aware of it, but the numb half of her brain just hadn't been able to express her appreciation. And now she was kicking

172

herself for not realising he'd been worried about her, too.

"You're the best Christmas present I could ever have, Tim," she whispered, not being able to put anything more into words.

And the way her husband looked at her and then held her, she knew their love was such that she didn't have to explain any more.

A FTER the previous night's rain, Christmas morning dawned sunny, bright and cold. They always exchanged presents before breakfast, but Tim suggested they wait until the afternoon.

"Until after we've spoken with Tate, you mean?" They'd arranged to do that at three-thirty.

The Queen's speech was just ending when the doorbell rang, and Tim went to answer it.

"Don't be long," she called, switching on the computer, which was already set up in the conservatory. She couldn't wait to see Tate's face and hear his voice.

"Mum!"

She turned, and Tate was there in the flesh.

"Surprise!" He grinned.

"Oh, Tate!" she shrieked, and clung to him.

Over his shoulder, Tim was grinning. He'd known about Tate getting a flight back home for Christmas all along. But there were tears in his eyes, too.

"The new house is great, Mum," Tate said. "You're getting used to it now, I guess. And I'm loving that tree. We've never had a real one before, have we?"

Most things about this Christmas had turned out very different from usual, but that didn't make them any less special, she realised, as she switched out the lights on the tree before going up to bed. Life was all about change.

This year, alongside her nostalgia for the past, they'd made some new memories and started some new traditions to take into the future. But perhaps the most important lesson she'd learned this Christmas was to appreciate all the blessings she did have.

"You've been a fantastic tree." She touched a branch and was rewarded with the faint odour of fresh pine. "And you smell absolutely gorgeous!"

"So do you, my love," Tim said, tiptoeing in and pulling her close. "So do I take it we're having a real tree every year from now on . . .?"

"Yes, and no," she replied. "We'll have a real one, but hopefully it will be this same tree. I want to try to keep it going if I can. What about if we get a proper pot for it in the New Year sales? And while we're at the garden centre, it's time we started to think about what else we're going to do with the garden this summer . . ."

She drank in her husband's smile, while feeling her own heart lighten with each new plan for the future. ■